THE NEXT GENERATION®

ALL
GOOD
THINGS . . .

ALL

GOOD

THINGS . . .

A Novel by
Michael Jan Friedman

Based on ALL GOOD THINGS . . .
Written by
Ronald D. Moore & Brannon Braga

SIMON & SCHUSTER

LONDON·SYDNEY·NEW YORK·TOKYO·SINGAPORE·TORONTO

First published in Great Britain by Simon & Schuster Ltd, 1994
A Paramount Communications Company

Simon & Schuster Ltd
West Garden Place
Kendal Street
London W2 2AQ
Simon & Schuster of Australia Pty Ltd
Sydney

A CIP catalogue record for this book is available from the British Library.
ISBN: 0-671-71898-3

Printed in the U.S.A.

To Joan and Brett,
for understanding, past, present, and future.

ALL
GOOD
THINGS . . .

CHAPTER 1

He hated balalaika music, hated it with a passion. However, he would put up with it just this once. And not because he had to. He would put up with it specifically because he *didn't* have to.

As he sat at his solitary table on a candlelit balcony overlooking the beach, sipping at his vodka and pushing a pitted olive around his plate, a woman emerged from the dining room within.

By local standards, she was quite beautiful, with alabaster skin and pale blond hair woven into a bun. She wore a safari outfit, though she had probably never been on a safari in her theoretical life.

"The nights are beautiful here," she said.

He shrugged. "I suppose . . . if you like that sort of thing."

She gazed at him from under long, straw-colored lashes. "Don't you?"

"I guess I don't have much of an opinion," he admitted.

"How strange," she said. "An attractive man like yourself, alone on a night like this . . . usually has opinions about a great many things."

He smiled at her. "If I'm not mistaken, you came into this place with such a man. I'll bet he's wondering where you are even as we speak."

She moved and the moonlight glinted off her hair. "Perhaps he is. And he certainly does have his share of opinions. It's just that I'm a little tired of them."

"I see," he told her. "And now you'd prefer to hear some of mine."

"You're a very clever man," she observed. "You catch on quickly."

"Yes," he agreed. "I do. And for just a moment there, you were almost interesting. But . . ." He smiled politely. "I think that moment has passed."

The woman's eyes went wide. "How dare you . . . ?" she gasped. For a moment, she seemed on the verge of slapping him in the face. But in the end, she decided not to, and simply disappeared back into the dining room.

Oh well, he told himself. I guess that's the way the flaxen-haired tourist bounces.

Out of the corner of his eye, he saw two figures hopping around down below—removing their shoes, he gathered. As he watched, they slipped away from the mellow, orange circle of light that emanated from the tavern. One was male, one female; one broad-shouldered and big-boned, the other comparatively slender.

He knew them, of course. Knew them quite well, in fact.

2

They were both barefoot as they made their way along the margin of the sea, leaving wet footprints in the sand. From time to time, one of them would reach for the other's hand, then let it go again. It was obvious that they were still in the courting stage, feeling each other out, uncertain of how far to take this evening without overstepping some unstated boundary.

Such a waste of time. If they wanted to procreate, why not do so? Why this elaborate and confusing ritual, when they could be spending their time on more valuable pursuits? On the improvement of their backward race, for example?

But no. Not them. All they could think of was their own, petty concerns. He shivered at the inanity of it. At the sheer, unmitigated ego—a subject on which he was quite the expert.

The breeze ruffled the stars in the clear night sky, bringing him the primitive scent of the prize-winning goulash cooking in the kitchen below. It would have made his mouth water, if his mouth had had the prospensity to do such things.

Of course, it didn't. But then, he wasn't really here to soak up the scenery—or the local vodka, for that matter. He was making his plans—weaving his web like a big, fat, black spider, strand by dangerous strand.

And the best part was they had no idea what was coming . . . no idea how it would affect their puny lives, or what role he would play in it. They didn't even know he was here in their holodeck fantasy, or they would have put their shoes back on and railed at him to leave them alone.

Humans liked their privacy. They liked it a lot. And

3

even if these two weren't completely human, they still shared that particular trait.

So he remained a part of the scenery and tolerated the balalaika music. Soon enough, he consoled himself, they'd be dancing to *his* tune. And not just the two fainthearted lovers on the beach, but the whole kaboodle of them.

A waiter emerged from the dining room. "May I get you something more?" the man asked, in his twentieth-century Russian dialect. "Some dessert, perhaps? We have lovely fruit."

He looked up at the waiter. "No, thank you," he replied, in the same dialect. "I'll be leaving in a moment. Places to go, things to do, Starfleet officers to torment. You know how it is."

The waiter didn't, of course, so he just smiled. "If you are leaving," the man suggested, "may I bring you your bill?"

He nodded. "Why not? We've all got to pay the piper sometime, don't we?" He frowned as the music swelled to even more infuriating levels. "Or in this case, the damned balalaika player."

According to the ship's computer, the Eskimos of Earth's North American continent had sixteen words for *snow*. In that light, it had always seemed strange to Worf that his own people, the Klingons, should have but one word for *honor*.

The word was *batlh*. And for all its simplicity, it was forced to cover a wide variety of situations.

For instance, there was the sense of honor that accompanied a promise kept, or a job well done. There was the standard of honor that encouraged warriors to die bravely. And there was the principle of honor that presided over a government, or a ship, or even a marriage bed, when all parties dealt openly and fairly with one another.

It was this last sort that occupied Worf's mind as he escorted Deanna Troi from one of the *Enterprise*'s holodecks. For as much as he enjoyed her company, it did not come without its share of . . . inconveniences.

"That was an incredible program," said Deanna, smiling as she looked up at him.

The Klingon nodded. "I am glad you approve. I have always found the Black Sea at night to be a most . . . stimulating experience."

His companion rolled her eyes at him as they walked down the stark, metallic corridor. He wondered what he had said to occasion such a reaction.

"Worf," she moaned, "we were strolling barefoot along the beach while balalaika music played in the air. A sea breeze washing over us . . . stars in the sky . . . a full moon rising . . . and the most you can say is 'stimulating'?"

He groped for a more appropriate response. "It was . . . *very* stimulating? *Extremely* stimulating?"

Deanna shook her head in mock disapproval as they approached a turbolift. "Honestly, Worf. If you weren't such a delightful companion . . ."

Entering the lift, she instructed it to take them to deck eight. As the doors closed, the Klingon looked at her. She looked back. And, unable to help himself, he looked away.

Strange, wasn't it? He would rather face a roomful of Romulans than speak of certain personal concerns . . . even with someone like Deanna, who was bound to understand them. Hell's blasted battleground . . . if she didn't, who would?

"The truth is," said the Betazoid, obviously changing the subject for his benefit, "I don't spend nearly enough time in the holodecks. I should take my own advice and use them to relax."

Worf thought about his holodeck calisthenics program. "Most times," he confessed, "I use them for other things besides relaxing."

Deanna chuckled softly. "Yes," she said. "I've heard." As the doors opened, depositing them on deck eight, they stepped out. The entrance to her quarters was just opposite the lift.

"Next time," she went on, *"I'll* choose the program. If you like the Black Sea, you're going to love Lake Cataria on Betazed. Especially the aurora . . . the way it folds and twists and changes from blue to violet to a sullen orange. And the scents that come out of the forest that surrounds the lake . . . You'd really enjoy it."

For a moment, as they stood outside her suite, their eyes met and established a bond. Worf basked in the scent of her, in her warmth, in her beauty. He felt his discomfort slip away . . . and decided this was as good a time as any to mention his misgivings.

"Deanna," he began, "perhaps before there is a 'next time,' we should discuss . . . Commander Riker."

She grinned playfully. "Why? Will he be coming along?"

Worf frowned. This was a serious matter, and she didn't seem inclined to make it any easier for him.

"No," he said. "But I do not wish to . . . I mean, it would be unfortunate if he . . ." He took a breath, started again. "If you and I are going to continue to . . . to . . ." He gave up. "I do not want to hurt his feelings."

Deanna took his hands in hers. "Worf . . . I think it's all right to concentrate on *our* feelings. Yours . . . and mine."

Her smile was contagious. Gazing into her eyes, reassured, he began to forget about Commander Riker —and everything else in the world. As he leaned over to kiss her, she lifted her lips to his.

But before they could touch, the turbolift doors opened with a hiss—and the captain burst out of them. Worf stared in disbelief. Not only was Picard uncharacteristically wide-eyed with panic, he was wearing nothing but a blue-and-white striped bathrobe!

"Counselor!" cried the captain.

Coming between her and Worf, apparently oblivious of what he had just interrupted, Picard gripped Deanna by her arms.

"What's today's date? The *date?"* he demanded.

"Stardate four-seven-nine-eight-eight," the Klingon said, interjecting the answer.

Letting go of the Betazoid, Picard turned away from them and mulled it over. He seemed to be having enormous difficulty, considering the simplicity of the concept.

"Four-seven-nine-eight-eight . . ." the captain echoed.

Deanna looked at him. "Sir, what's wrong?"

Picard's brow furrowed. "I'm not sure," he told her. "I don't know how . . . or why, but . . ." He shook his head. "I believe I'm moving back and forth through time."

A chill ran up along Worf's spine. His relationship with Deanna would have to resume its progress some other time. It was clear what honor demanded of him.

Looking up at the intercom grid, he called on Commander Riker.

CHAPTER 2

As Worf entered his quarters, he saw that the light was on in Alexander's room. And that Alexander himself was at his desk, studying his monitor.

The security chief temporarily put aside his concern for the captain's condition and approached his son. Noticing him, Alexander looked up and smiled. He had the smell of cookies and milk about him, though a human might not have noticed.

"Hi, Father."

Worf didn't smile back. It was late—well after ten o'clock.

"Alexander . . . should you not be in bed?"

The boy shrugged. "I have an organic-chemistry exam tomorrow morning, and there are a few things I'm still fuzzy on."

The security chief grunted and moved to his own room. He could hardly fault Alexander for taking his studies so seriously. What's more, he felt badly that he hadn't spent much time helping with them lately.

However, he'd had other things on his mind. Things that he could not seem to ignore. Like Deanna.

Removing his casual clothes, he changed into his uniform and noted how comfortable it made him feel—more so than any other garb. Commander Riker had ordered several scans done, in order to determine if the captain had indeed left the ship for some period of time. He was to report to the bridge as soon as he was properly attired.

As he reached for his heavy, ceremonial sash, he saw Alexander standing at the threshold. He was still smiling. "You were with Deanna, huh?"

Worf gave his son a quizzical look. "What makes you say that?"

"I can always tell," the boy replied—and padded back to his room on bare feet.

The security chief followed him there. "What do you mean, you can 'always tell'?" he asked.

Alexander peered at his monitor. "She puts you in a good mood. Whenever you spend time together, you come back with a smile on your face."

Worf straightened. "I was not smiling when I came in the door."

His son turned to him. "Dad . . . I know when you're smiling, even when no one else does." He paused. "You like her. It's obvious."

The Klingon wasn't comfortable admitting it—but he couldn't deny Alexander's observation altogether. "Counselor Troi is a . . . close friend," he said. "That is all."

The boy nodded. "Right." And without another word, he went back to his studies.

Worf thought for a moment. It had not been so long since Alexander's mother had died from an assassin's attack—and right before the boy's eyes. He did not wish to cause his son any more trauma than was necessary.

And yet, if his relationship with the counselor continued in the direction it was going in . . . well, it would be unfair not to sound the boy out on the subject. After all, his life would be affected as well.

"But if that were *not* the case," the security chief said, opening the conversation again, "if Deanna were more than a friend to me . . . how would you feel about that?"

Alexander looked up with barely contained excitement. "You mean it? You're going to start seeing her romantically?"

The Klingon held up a hand. "I did not say that. I was merely posing a . . . hypothetical situation."

The boy tried out the word. "Hypo . . . thetical. That means it's possible, right?"

Worf shrugged. "Well . . . yes."

Alexander considered the prospect. When he responded, it was with great seriousness. "Then . . . hypothetically, you understand . . . I would approve."

The Klingon nodded. He was greatly pleased, even if he didn't show it. "I will see you later," he assured the boy. "After I have performed some special scans." He paused, for effect. "And when I come back this time, I expect you to be in bed—sleeping."

His son nodded. "Yes, sir." Then, almost as an afterthought: "And say hi to Counselor Troi for me."

Worf scowled. He didn't like being teased, even by Alexander.

"I will," he said, and departed for the bridge.

"The Iron Feather?" Geordi repeated. "Interesting title."

"Yes," said Data, who was walking along beside him in the gently curving corridor. His voice echoed slightly from bulkhead to bulkhead. "It is the latest work by Christian McCloy . . . the story of one man's journey of self-discovery set against the chaos of mid–twenty-first-century Earth."

"The post-atomic horror," the chief engineer noted. He grimaced. "Not my favorite period in Terran history."

"Nor mine," agreed the android. "However, I found it to be a most engrossing work of fiction. I highly recommend it."

Geordi nodded. "I see. And is there a holodeck version?"

"I do not believe so," Data replied.

In that case, the human wasn't all that interested. But he didn't want to offend his companion, so he didn't say that.

"You know, Data, I think I'd rather be in the story than just read about it. So thanks for the offer, but I'll take a rain check."

The android glanced at him. For a moment, the engineer expected to have to explain his colloquialism. Then Data turned away again, so apparently no explanation was needed.

Without question, Geordi's artificial friend had come a long way since he'd first set foot on the *Enterprise.* For one thing, he no longer took people's words so literally. And for another, his mastery of behavioral nuances was such that . . . sometimes . . . one could almost forget he was an android.

As they stopped by a turbolift, Data turned to him again. "Although I have found the holodeck to be a most effective means of expanding my understanding of existing works, I still find the experience of reading the author's original narrative to be the most—"

He was interrupted by the swish of the opening lift doors. *To be continued,* Geordi mused—*whether I like it or not.*

As they stepped in, however, they saw that Worf was already in the compartment. That raised a question in the engineer's mind.

"What's wrong?" he asked the security chief.

Worf frowned. "How do you know that something is wrong?"

"I believe," Data interjected, "it has something to do with your being in uniform, when your next tour of duty is several hours from now."

Geordi nodded. "Exactly."

The Klingon's frown deepened. "It is the captain," he said at last. "He was in the corridor just a little while ago. Wandering about in his bathrobe."

The engineer couldn't believe it. "Really?"

Worf nodded. "He asked what stardate it was. As if he had no idea."

"That does not sound like Captain Picard," the android noted. "Has it been determined what was wrong with him?"

The security chief shook his head. "Not yet. Counselor Troi is with him now." He paused. "I think that is all I should say. After all, there are questions of privacy here and—"

Geordi held up his hand. "Go no further. I understand, Worf."

And he did. But he resolved to look in on the captain as soon as his own tour was over. With any luck, this incident would turn out to be nothing . . . but one never knew.

CHAPTER 3

Picard stared into the wispy vapors coming up from his tea. So far, he hadn't touched the stuff—and not because it wasn't to his liking. After all, Earl Grey was his favorite blend.

He was simply too distracted to think much about drinking anything. He had too much else on his mind.

"It was," he blurted, "as though I had physically left the ship and gone to another time and place. I was in the past. . . ."

He shook his head. Why couldn't he get a better handle on what had happened? It seemed to be on the brink of his consciousness, teasing him . . . but when he reached for it, it slipped away.

Deanna sat on the other side of the smooth, dark coffee table that her mother had given her as a gift. The counselor's incredulity was visible only in the slightest wrinkling of the skin above the bridge of her nose. Outside of that, she seemed completely nonjudgmental.

"Can you describe where you were?" she asked. "What it looked like?"

The captain sighed as the scent of the tea teased his nostrils. "It's all so difficult to nail down," he told her. "Like the details of a nightmare after you've woken up."

"What *can* you remember?" the Betazoid prodded carefully.

Picard concentrated. "It was years ago . . . before I took command of the *Enterprise*. I was talking with someone . . . I don't remember who. It was dark outside. . . ."

The half-formed image lingered before his mind's eye. His head hurt with the effort of trying to refine it, to understand it.

"But then . . ." he began.

"Yes?" said Deanna.

He struggled with it. "Then everything changed. I wasn't in the past any longer. I was an old man, in the future. I was doing something . . . something outside." He cursed softly. "What was it?"

Abruptly, he realized that his fingers were moving, as if of their own accord. They were rubbing together. But why? For what purpose?

Then the image was gone. "Sorry," he told the counselor, bowing his head. "I just can't remember."

Deanna smiled compassionately. "It's all right," she assured him. And then, as gently as she could manage: "Captain . . . have you considered the possibility that this was just a dream?"

Picard looked up. "No. It was more than a dream," he said, with a certainty that took him by surprise. "The smells and the sounds . . . the way things felt to the touch . . . they escape me now, but at the time it was all very real."

The Betazoid accepted the statement with equanimity. "How long did you stay in each of these time periods?" she inquired, apparently taking a different tack. "Did it seem like minutes . . . hours?"

The captain thought about it. "I'm not sure," he concluded after a moment. "At first . . . at first there was a moment of confusion, of disorientation. I wasn't sure where I was. But that passed. . . ." He frowned. "And then I felt perfectly natural . . . as though I belonged in that time." He grunted. "But I can't remember now how long I stayed there."

It was all so frustrating. The counselor sensed it, too, because she didn't press him any further.

"I know," he told her. "This doesn't make much sense. It's a set of feelings more than a distinct memory."

"It's all right," said Deanna. "Maybe it would be easier to try identifying specific symbols. Can you remember anything you *saw* . . . anything at all? An object, a building, perhaps . . . ?"

He took a breath, let it out. "No," he answered finally. "Nothing."

Finally, feeling that he'd run up against a wall, Picard focused again on his tea. It was no longer producing any vapors. Obviously, he had let it sit too long.

The counselor had noticed as well, it seemed. "Here," she said, reaching across the table. "Let me have your cup. I'll get you some more."

"Thank you," he said. Picking up the smooth, ceramic cup and its matching saucer, he extended them to her . . .

. . . and took hold of the rough-skinned grapevine. Suddenly, Picard had the strangest feeling that he had been reaching for something else.

For a moment, he felt lost, out of place. Peering out from under the brim of his straw hat, he took in the long, graceful contours of his family vineyard. He saw the fog lifting off them in the low rays of the rising sun . . . smelled the richness of the soil . . . heard the buzz of flying insects . . . and confirmed that he was just where he was supposed to be.

Still, for just a second there, it seemed to him he was in another place altogether. He wasn't sure where, or even when, but . . . oh, what the hell. When people aged, their minds were allowed to wander a bit.

There was nothing wrong with that, was there? With all the thinking his mind had done, it had earned a little excursion now and then.

Concentrating on the vine in his hand, he appraised it with the trained eye of someone who had grown up under the tutelage of expert vintners. Then, reaching for a pair of pruning shears, he snipped off a few stray branches. Certainly, he could have hired others to do this work—but it felt good to be useful. And Lord knew, he wasn't qualified to do much else these days.

"Captain Picard to the bridge!" a voice rang out.

Picard could scarcely believe his ears. He looked up from his work and squinted.

To his surprise, there was someone standing there in the vineyard—though the figure was silhouetted in the early-morning sun, so he couldn't tell who it was right away. Then, as he shaded his eyes, he made out a familiar and welcome visage.

"Geordi," he whispered. "Geordi La Forge."

His former chief engineer smiled with genuine enthusiasm as he approached. "Sir, I think we have a problem with the warp core, or the phase inducers, or some other damn thing. It'd normally take days to repair—but if you need me to, I can fix it in a few minutes. No—make that a few seconds. And if you want, I can run a few diagnostics while I'm at it as well."

The older man stood, though not without a bit of difficulty. "Damn," he said, scratching at his bearded chin. "It's really you, isn't it?"

La Forge was wearing civilian clothes—and why shouldn't he? He had left Starfleet a good many years ago, though not as many as Picard himself. Also, the man's VISOR was gone—replaced by artificial eyes—and with his face rounded by age, and punctuated with a gray mustache, he was no longer the bushy-tailed young officer that the captain had known.

But then, time had passed for both of them. So much time, in fact, that it was depressing to think about it.

La Forge held out his hand. Picard grasped it with all the strength he could muster—which wasn't much, anymore.

"Hello, Captain," said his visitor. "Or should I make that Ambassador?"

Picard snorted. "It hasn't been *Ambassador* for a while either."

The younger man shrugged. "How about Mr. Picard?"

"How about *Jean-Luc?*" countered the vintner.

La Forge looked at him askance. His eyes glinted. "I don't know if I can get used to that, but I'll give it a shot."

For a long moment, they stood in the slanting rays of the sun, each taking in the sight of an old friend and comrade. Picard was the first to break the silence.

"Good lord, Geordi. How long has it been?"

La Forge grunted. "Oh . . . about nine years."

"No, no . . . I mean, since you called me *Captain* last? When was the last time we were all together . . . on the *Enterprise?*"

It took La Forge a little longer to answer that question. "Close to twenty-five years," he decided.

Picard shook his head. "Twenty-five years . . ." He smiled. "Time's been good to you, Commander."

The younger man patted his middle. "It's been a little *too* good to me in some places." He took a look around, his gaze finally fixing itself on the gardening tools that Picard had lugged out here—just as he did every morning. They were stacked just a few meters away.

"Can I give you a hand, sir?"

The older man shrugged. "Oh, I'm just tying some vines. I can handle it on my own."

La Forge knelt down anyway and examined one of the vines.

"Looks like you've got leaf miners," he announced after a second or two. "You might want to use a spray on them."

Picard looked at him. "What do *you* know about leaf miners?" he asked, full of curiosity.

20

To his knowledge, La Forge had never set foot in the ship's botanical garden—much less acquainted himself with Terran parasites. He'd been far too busy running herd over the ship's engines.

"My wife is quite a gardener," La Forge explained. "I've picked up a little bit of it. I mean . . . when you live with somebody who eats and breathes the stuff, it's hard not to. Just the other day, she spent hours planting a single flower. Something real fragile . . . a *b'lednaya*, I think she called it."

Without asking permission, he picked up a small length of shielded wire off the ground and began tying some of the vines. Satisfied—and yes, surprised—that his friend was taking the proper care, Picard knelt down beside him.

"How is Leah?" he asked.

La Forge chuckled softly. "Busier than anyone has a right to be—even when she's *not* planting flowers. She's just been made director of the Daystrom Institute. That means she'll be working harder than ever—but it's something she's always wanted."

Picard nodded, duly impressed. "The Daystrom Institute, eh? And what about the little ones . . . Bret and Alandra? And, er . . ." He tried to remember the last one's name.

Fortunately, his companion supplied it. "And *Sidney*. They're not so little anymore, Captain. Bret's applying to Starfleet Academy next year. His teachers think he'll make it, too—if he can beef up a little more on his quantum mechanics."

The older man swore under his breath. "Incredible,"

he remarked. Then, looking up at his visitor: "So what brings you here?"

La Forge kept his eyes focused on the vines he was tying. "Oh . . . I just thought I'd drop by. You know how it is. I'd been thinking about the old days on the *Enterprise,* how much fun we used to have . . . and anyway, I was in the neighborhood . . ."

Picard smelled a rat. "Don't give me that," he rasped. "You don't make the trip from Rigel Three to Earth just to . . . to drop by. It's . . ." He tried to think of how many light-years, but finally gave up. "A long way," he finished lamely.

La Forge swallowed. He was no more skilled at deception now than he had been a quarter of a century ago.

"Yes," he agreed. "I suppose it is."

Picard eyed him. "So you've heard," he pressed.

The younger man turned to him. "Well," he confessed, "Leah has a few friends at Starfleet medical, you know? And word has a way of getting around . . . especially when it concerns someone of your stature."

Picard flushed with indignation. "I'm not an invalid, you know. Irumodic syndrome can take years to run its course."

La Forge nodded. "I know. But when I heard, I just . . . I wanted to come by all the same."

The older man looked at his friend for a moment. La Forge hadn't meant to offend him . . . just to lend some support. Certainly, he didn't deserve to be condemned for that.

When Picard spoke again, his voice was softer, less

cantankerous. "Well," he said, "as long as you're here, you can help me carry in some of these tools."

La Forge grinned. "It's a deal," he said.

Awkwardly, and not without some pain, Picard got to his feet. "My cooking may not be up to Leah's standards," he warned. "But I can still make a decent cup of tea."

Grabbing an armful of his farming implements, he saw his visitor do the same. Together, they started walking toward the house where Picard had been raised. It was barely visible around the bend of the hill.

"By the way," said the vintner, "I read your last novel. Not bad, not bad at all."

"Really?" replied La Forge. Like a great many authors before him, there was something of the small child about him, seeking approval.

The captain nodded. "Really. It had a certain, er . . . authenticity to it that I found quite refreshing. Of course, I didn't like the main character all that much . . . what was his name?"

"Patrick."

"Patrick, of course. Not quite the fellow I would have chosen to run *my* ship. But that's just my own, personal . . ."

Suddenly, Picard stopped dead in his tracks. Standing in the vineyards, not fifty meters away, was a trio of the sorriest, scraggliest excuses for human beings that he'd ever seen.

He didn't recognize any of them. In fact, he'd never seen them before in his life. So what in blazes were they doing in his vineyard?

Before he could ask them that question, they began pointing at him—pointing and jeering. Then shouting at the tops of their lungs, as if they found something amusing about him. Picard suppressed his indignation.

Out of the corner of his eye, he could see his companion looking at him. He looked concerned.

"Captain," asked La Forge, "are you all right?"

"I'm fine," said Picard, keeping his eyes on the intruders. "I just want to know what these people are doing in my vineyard. . . ."

"Captain?"

Picard turned at the sound of the shuttle pilot's voice. "Yes, Lieutenant?" he muttered.

"Are you all right, sir?"

He wasn't sure. He seemed to have drifted off—but not merely figuratively. It was almost as if he'd been somewhere else until just this second . . . somewhere very different from the shuttlecraft *Galileo*.

But of course, that was ridiculous. For the last several minutes, he'd been sitting in the copilot's seat of the small, crisp-looking craft, making the brief trip from the shipyard offices to his new command.

Perhaps he was just nervous, he told himself. After all, it had been several years since he'd sat in the center seat of a starship—and the assignment he was headed for was significantly more demanding than the *Stargazer* had been.

"Sir?" prodded the pilot, who was also to be one of his senior officers when he took command.

Picard turned to her, noting the way her prickly,

no-nonsense attitude clashed with her striking good looks. Her skin was tinted a pale green by the craft's interior lighting; it accentuated the green of her eyes.

He smiled, a little embarrassed. "I'm sorry, Lieutenant Yar. My mind seems to have wandered for a moment. What was it you were saying?"

She seemed to relax a bit. "I was asking if you'd ever been aboard a Galaxy-class starship before, sir."

Picard focused his mind on answering the question. Though he still had the nagging sensation that he'd left something unfinished somewhere, he tried to ignore it.

"No," he replied. "I'm, of course, very familiar with the blueprints and specifications . . . and I've seen holograms of its performance projections . . . but this will be my first time aboard."

The young woman smiled—an expression of pride more than one of pleasure. "Well then, sir, if I may be so bold . . . you're in for a treat. The *Enterprise* is quite a ship."

The captain nodded. "I'm sure she is."

Of course, he couldn't see it yet, with all the yard's other ships hovering in the way like a pack of high-tech herd animals. But he would get an eyeful of the *Enterprise* soon enough.

As it was, he found Lieutenant Yar's face much more interesting. There was something about it that seemed . . . familiar, he thought, even though he was only noticing it now for the first time.

Perhaps it was just one of those faces. He was relatively certain he had never met her before today. Or had he?

After a moment, Yar seemed to notice that he was scrutinizing her. She glanced back at him.

"Sir?" A pause. "Have I done something wrong?" she asked.

"No," he said. "Of course not, Lieutenant."

He was sorry for the misconception he'd caused. No matter how curious he was, it had been wrong of him to stare.

"You just seem familiar to me," he explained further. "I was wondering if we had run into one another on a prior occasion."

The woman's brow wrinkled. "I don't think so," she replied.

Picard nodded. "No," he agreed. "Perhaps not."

Yar returned her attention to her control console. A second later, the communications panel beeped. She hit the appropriate control pad.

"Enterprise to shuttlecraft *Galileo,"* announced the ship's officer in charge of shuttle traffic. "You are cleared for arrival in shuttlebay two."

The lieutenant's response was crisp and professional: "Acknowledged, *Enterprise."*

Working her controls for a moment, she pointed to a spot dead ahead, between two smaller starships. The captain craned his neck to follow her gesture, but he couldn't see anything yet from where he was sitting.

"There she is," said Yar.

A moment later, he saw what she was talking about, as the Galaxy-class *Enterprise* swam into view. Picard felt his heart skip as he took in the majesty and the grace and the magnitude of her.

Her saucer section alone could accommodate more than a thousand people, he had learned. And her nacelles—positioned underneath the ship, where the *Stargazer*'s had been placed above—were not only elegant, but highly efficient. Even in the midst of all the other half-ready vessels in the yard, she seemed to stand out—to shine.

"She's beautiful," he commented, without intending to. And then, because the word didn't seem to praise her enough: "Absolutely breathtaking."

The lieutenant nodded. "She certainly is. . . ."

". . . Captain?"

Picard blinked. He was in Deanna's quarters again, holding out his ceramic cup full of cold tea. The counselor herself was staring at him, her dark eyes fixed on his—as if he'd just said or done something entirely inappropriate. And there was a feeling in his stomach the likes of which he'd never felt before.

"Tasha," he muttered, his eyes going in and out of focus.

"I beg your pardon?" responded Deanna.

"Tasha," he repeated dully, his own voice sounding strange in his ears. "I was just with Tasha, in the shuttle. . . ."

Suddenly, it was all too much for him. His accumulated feelings of disorientation swept over him like a tidal wave, threatening to crush him. Somewhere off in the distance, he heard the sound of his cup shattering on the table.

In what seemed like a long, dizzying fall, Picard slumped back into his chair. His skull was ringing furiously, like a thousand chiming clocks. He put his hands to his ears in an attempt to shut them out, but he couldn't. They were too loud, too insistent.

"Captain?" came a cry, taut with concern. And again, tighter still: "Captain?"

"I . . ." he began. "I . . . can't . . ."

There was a dull sound—like a hand hitting something hard, something metallic. His stomach lurched.

"Troi to Dr. Crusher." The words seemed at once very close and very far away. "Something's wrong with the captain. We're on our way to sickbay."

And then he blacked out altogether.

CHAPTER 4

Dr. Beverly Crusher had seen her friend, the captain, in many a narrow strait. However, she had never seen him look quite so meek or helpless as he did now.

Sitting in his robe on the biobed in front of her, Jean-Luc was just staring into space, and had been for nearly a minute. He seemed oblivious of the doctors and nurses going about their business elsewhere in sickbay.

It made her feel helpless, too—because even after the battery of brain-activity tests she'd put him through, she still couldn't figure out what was wrong with him. Sighing, she completed one last scan with her tricorder and considered the results.

Troi, who was standing at the foot of the bed, looked at the doctor hopefully. Unfortunately, Crusher would have to dash that hope.

"I don't see anything that might cause hallucinations or a psychogenic reaction," she said.

The captain turned to her. "Nothing?"

"Nothing," echoed the doctor.

"Is there any indication of temporal displacement?" queried Troi. "Anything that might shed some light on the problem?"

Crusher shook her head. "Not that I can see. Usually, a temporal shift would leave some kind of trypamine residue in the cerebral cortex. But the scans didn't find any."

Gently, she put her hand on Jean-Luc's shoulder. He half-smiled at the gesture, but his mind was clearly on his troubles.

"Frankly," she said, trying to lighten things up a bit, "I think you just enjoy waking everyone up in the middle of the night."

The captain looked at her. He seemed grateful for her effort to ease the considerable tension.

"Actually," he replied, picking up on her gibe, "I *enjoy* running around the ship in my bare feet. I find it . . ." He pretended to search for the right word. "Invigorating," he decided at last.

Now it was the doctor's turn to smile. "No doubt you do."

"Dr. Crusher?"

The chief medical officer turned. Alissa Ogawa, one of her nurses, was headed this way with a padd. Ogawa was six months pregnant and looked every minute of it.

"Here are the biospectral test results," said the nurse.

"Thanks, Alissa," said Crusher.

Smiling, Ogawa crossed sickbay to attend to other things—and the doctor looked over the results displayed on the padd. Finally, satisfied that there could be no error, she turned to her patient, who had been watching her as she went over the data.

"And?" he asked.

"Well," she told him, "your blood-gas analysis is consistent with someone who's been breathing the ship's air for weeks. If you'd been somewhere else, there would be some indication of a change in your dissolved oxygen levels—but there isn't any such indication. You haven't left the *Enterprise*, Jean-Luc. Not as far as I can tell."

He frowned. "I don't understand," he said. He got that faraway look again—the one that tore at Crusher's heart. Unfortunately, the doctor thought, that wasn't the worst news she would give him today.

Turning to Troi, she asked, "Counselor . . . would you be good enough to excuse us for a moment?"

The Betazoid looked a little surprised, but she took the request in stride. "Of course," she replied. And then, to the captain: "I'll look in on you a little later."

Jean-Luc nodded—but his gaze was fixed on the doctor now. He, too, wondered what kind of remarks required such privacy.

As Troi headed for the exit, Crusher met his scrutiny. This wasn't going to be easy, she told herself. But, as his doctor, she had to tell him.

"Jean-Luc," she began, "our scans didn't show any evidence of Irumodic syndrome. But it did reveal a particular kind of defect in your parietal lobe." She paused, choosing her words carefully. "It's the kind of defect that could make you susceptible to several neurological disorders later in life . . . *including* Irumodic syndrome."

31

The captain absorbed the news. "I see," he said.

Until this moment, he had been dealing only with something he'd experienced elsewhere—more than likely, it seemed, in a particularly vivid nightmare. Now the nightmare—or at least this one aspect of it—was invading his *real* world.

Still, whatever dark prospects he contemplated, he kept them to himself. Outwardly, he didn't show the least sign of self-pity.

"Now," she continued, "it's possible you could have that defect for the rest of your life without developing a problem. And even if the syndrome does develop, many people lead perfectly normal lives for a long time after its onset."

Jean-Luc smiled wryly—even courageously. "Then why," he asked, "do you look like you've just signed my death sentence?"

He said it with a hint of a smile, so she wouldn't get the wrong idea. Just as she had tried to break the tension earlier, he was trying his best to break it now.

After all, he knew that *she* would not be pleased about this either. Not only was she his physician, she was his friend. And at times, she had been on the verge of becoming something even more.

"Sorry," said Crusher, unable to quite bring herself to smile with him. "I guess . . . this has caught me off guard."

The captain took a contemplative breath and let it out. "Well, it'll either happen or it won't. However, since we have no control over it, there's no point in worrying." He looked at her with something akin to defiance in his eyes. "Besides," he added, "something tells me you're going to have to put up with me for a very long time."

The doctor shrugged. "It won't be easy," she told him, attempting to match his attitude, "but I'll manage."

She wanted to say more, but she was interrupted by the entrance of First Officer Will Riker. Crossing sickbay in several long strides, he looked as serious as Crusher felt. Of course, Riker didn't know anything about the potential for Irumodic syndrome, which worried the doctor even more than Jean-Luc's current malady.

The captain eyed his second-in-command. "Well?" he inquired. "Did Worf find anything?"

Riker shook his head. "No, sir. His security scans came up negative." He held his hands out in a gesture of apology. "They're checking the sensor logs . . . but there's still no indication that you left the ship."

Jean-Luc slipped off the biobed and harrumphed. "It wasn't a dream," he insisted. "Something *did* happen."

Abruptly, they were interrupted by a voice on the intercom net. "Worf to Captain Picard."

The captain looked up. "Go ahead, Lieutenant."

"Sir, there is an incoming transmission from Admiral Nakamura. It is a Priority One message."

Priority One? Crusher knew that Starfleet didn't use that designation lightly.

Jean-Luc turned to her. "Beverly?"

She knew what he wanted—and she had no objections. "Go ahead," she said. "Use it if you like."

The captain nodded by way of a thank-you. "Mr.

Worf," he instructed, "route the communication through to Dr. Crusher's office."

"Aye, sir," replied the Klingon. "Rerouting . . ."

As Jean-Luc started across sickbay, the chief medical officer sighed. She hoped that Nakamura didn't want too much of the captain. It wasn't as if he didn't have *enough* on his mind.

CHAPTER 5

Entering the doctor's office, Picard sat down at her desk and activated the desktop monitor. After a moment, the solemn visage of Admiral Nakamura appeared on the screen.

"Captain," said the admiral.

"Admiral," returned Picard. One didn't drag out Priority One messages with small talk.

Nakamura shifted slightly in his chair. "Jean-Luc, I'm initiating a fleetwide yellow alert. Starfleet intelligence has picked up some disturbing reports from the Romulan Empire."

"What sort of news?" asked the captain.

The admiral frowned. "It appears that they're mobilizing for something. At least thirty Warbirds have been pulled from other assignments and are heading for the Neutral Zone."

That was disturbing news indeed. "Is there any indication why they would make such a blatantly aggressive move, Admiral?"

"Perhaps," said Nakamura. "Our operatives on Romulus have indicated that something is happening *in* the Neutral Zone—specifically, in the Devron system. Our own long-range scans have picked up some kind of spatial anomaly in the area, but we can't tell what it is—or why the Romulans might have taken an interest in it."

"I see," responded Picard. "And what are our orders?"

The admiral scowled. "As you can imagine, this is a delicate situation. I'm deploying fifteen starships along our side of the Neutral Zone. And I want you to go there as well—to see if you can find out what's going on in the Devron system."

The captain pondered his instructions. "Am I authorized to enter the Zone?" he inquired.

Nakamura shook his head. "Not yet. Wait and see what the Romulans do. You can conduct long-range scans, send probes if you wish . . . but don't cross the border unless they cross it *first.*"

"Understood," Picard assured him.

"Good luck," said the admiral. And with that, his image vanished, replaced with the official insignia of Starfleet.

Turning off the monitor, the captain stood . . .

. . . and felt a sudden wave of vertigo wash over him. He felt himself falling . . . falling . . . reaching out . . . until he was caught by a pair of strong arms.

Looking up, he saw that it was La Forge who had rescued him. The man's face was puckered with concern.

"Captain . . . what's wrong?" he asked.

With his friend's help, Picard steadied himself and looked around. His family's vineyard seem to stretch out forever in every direction. But . . . that wasn't *right,* was it? He didn't belong in the vineyard . . . or didn't . . .

"Is something wrong, sir?" pressed La Forge.

The older man tried to think. "I don't know," he responded. "I . . . I wasn't here a moment ago. . . ."

His visitor's worry lines deepened. "What do you mean? You've been right here with me, sir."

Picard groped for an answer. He tried to concentrate, to remember . . . but the damned Irumodic syndrome kept dragging down his every effort.

If only he were younger. If only his mind hadn't deteriorated. If only . . .

Stop it, he told himself. You're not going to get anywhere feeling sorry for yourself. Now, what happened to you? Try to remember, dammit.

"No," he said at last. "I wasn't here. I was somewhere else . . . a long time ago." He concentrated harder. "I was talking to someone. . . ."

And then it came to him. *Beverly* . . .

"Beverly was there."

He looked up at La Forge and saw an expression of disbelief. Picard's former comrade was beginning to wonder if the old man was losing it. It was evident in his eyes, even if they had been created in a lab somewhere.

"It's okay, Captain." He took hold of the vintner's arm. "Everything's going to be all right."

Flushed with anger, Picard pulled his arm away. "I am

not *senile.* It happened, I tell you. I was here, with you . . . and then I was in another place . . ." But where was it?

Again, he had a flash of insight. "It was . . . it was back on the *Enterprise!*" he croaked.

But how was that possible? He hadn't been on his old ship in a quarter of a century. And the more he thought about it, the more a host of doubts began to set in.

"At least," he went on, "I *think* it was the *Enterprise.* It seemed like sickbay . . . yes . . . but maybe it was a hospital . . . or . . ." He shrugged. How could he know? How could he be sure?

La Forge looked at him. "Captain, I think we should go back to the house. We could call a doctor. . . ."

Picard felt his anger crawl up into his throat, where it threatened to choke him. *"No,"* he grated. "I know what you're thinking. It's the Irumodic syndrome. It's beginning to . . . to affect the captain's mind. Well, it's not that. And . . . and I wasn't daydreaming either, dammit."

La Forge held up a hand for peace. "All right, sir . . . all right. Just calm down."

The older man felt the heat in his face start to ebb away. He straightened to his full height. "Apology accepted," he said, even though—technically—his visitor hadn't tendered one.

"So," La Forge probed, "something's happened. You've gone . . . er, somewhere else. And back again."

Picard nodded emphatically. "Damned right I have."

"Then . . ." The younger man appealed to him with his artificial eyes. "What do you want to do about it?"

The vintner considered the request, doing his best to seize on a course of action. Finally, one came to mind.

"I want to see *Data,*" he announced.

La Forge mulled it over. "I don't get it. Why Data?"

This was annoying. "Because I think he can help."

The younger man looked at him. "If you don't mind my asking, sir . . . help how?"

The anger exploded in him, almost as hot and bright as before. "I don't know!" roared Picard. "I don't know—but I want to see him, do you understand me?"

In the aftermath of the captain's outburst, La Forge hesitated. Obviously, he still wasn't putting much credence in anything the older man said. But in the end, he seemed to come to terms with the idea.

"Okay, sir. We'll go see Data, if that's what you want."

"It is," Picard confirmed.

The younger man's eyes narrowed. "He's still at Cambridge, isn't he?"

It was a good question. "Yes," said the vintner. "I think he . . ."

He never finished the sentence, distracted by a sudden movement in the corner of his eye. Turning toward it, he saw the intruders again—the scraggly, undernourished, hollow-eyed souls he'd noticed before.

But this time, there weren't three of them. There were *six.*

As before, they were jeering and pointing at Picard—though he hadn't the slightest idea why. Nor, for that matter, could he guess what they were doing here a second time.

He grabbed La Forge by the arm and, with an effort,

managed to turn him in the intruders' direction. "Do you see them?" he asked. "Do you?"

The other man looked out over the rolling vineyards. Then he looked back at Picard. "See *who?*"

The captain pointed to them. "They're out *there,*" he said. "Laughing at me. Why are they laughing, dammit?"

Why indeed? What was so funny? And who were they, anyway?

La Forge put his arm around Picard. It was a patently protective gesture. "Come on, Captain. Let's go see Data."

Picard started to protest—and then realized that the intruders were gone. There wasn't a sign of them—not a rag, not an echo. He scanned the vineyards in all directions, to no avail.

But how could they have disappeared so quickly? It was as if they'd dropped into a hole in the earth.

Or was it possible that he had imagined them after all? That they had never existed in the first place?

The older man swallowed. "Yes," he muttered. "Data . . . yes, of course."

And, feeling a little weak in the knees, he allowed his former comrade to guide him as they walked back toward the house.

Cambridge University hadn't changed much over the millennium or so since it was founded. At least, that was Geordi's understanding. Personally, he had been through the place only once before, on a family outing— and that was when he was very small.

Data's residence at the university was an old English manor house, built around the end of the sixteenth century. It had the smell of old wood about it. As Geordi approached the front door, with the captain at his side, he noticed the large brass knocker. It had been molded in the shape of a long-maned lion's head.

Geordi smiled. Here, as on the Picard family property, the primitive had been preserved and venerated. No doubt it was making the captain feel right at home.

He had been alarmed by Picard's behavior back in the vineyards. However, the captain hadn't seemed nearly so distracted on the way here. In fact, his excitement had seemed to focus his thoughts—to make him more lucid.

Why, there had been times on the trip from France to England when Geordi had completely forgotten that the man had Irumodic syndrome. Well, *almost* completely. There had been the incident with the poodle.

Reaching for the knocker, Geordi banged it a couple of times on the heavy wooden door. After a moment, the door opened. A dour-looking, red-faced woman somewhere in her fifties peered out at them. She looked broad enough to put the average Tellarite to shame.

"State your business," said the woman, with a heavy English accent. Her small, deep-set eyes announced that the two men were anything but welcome here, and dared them to say otherwise.

Still, they hadn't come all this way to be turned back now. "We're here to see Mr. Data," the former chief engineer explained. "My name is Geordi La Forge and this is Jean-Luc Picard. We're old friends of his."

The woman's eyes narrowed almost to slits. "I'm sure you are, sir. Everyone's friends with Mr. Data, it appears. But the professor's busy right now and can't be disturbed, y'see."

"But . . ."

"I'm sorry, sir."

As she began to close the door, Picard put his foot in the way. The woman glared at him.

"It's very important we see him immediately," he elaborated, glaring back. "We've come all the way from France."

The woman's expression indicated that she was not impressed. "Have you got wax in your ears?" she asked. "I told you he's *busy,* sir. If you wish to make an appointment, you'll have to go through the university— and let them decide how important it is. Now, don't make me call the constable on you, because I won't hesitate to—"

"Jessel? Who's at the door?"

Geordi would have known that voice anywhere— although there was a range of expressiveness in it that he hadn't heard before. The woman looked irritated. Obviously, she had no choice now but to announce their presence there.

"Just some *friends* of yours, sir," she called back into the house. "I told them to come back another time, when you're not so busy."

"Now, Jessel, I told you about frightening people away . . ."

As the sentence hung unfinished in the air, an inner door swung open—revealing none other than their old colleague, Data. Being an android, he hadn't aged over the years. However, there was a prominent streak of gray on one side of his head—not a natural streak, but one that looked as if a paintbrush had been taken to his head.

Data was wearing a cranberry-colored, synthetic-silk smoking jacket—the perfect complement to his surroundings. As he peered out at Geordi and the captain, his eyes seemed to go blank for a moment. Then, slowly, a smile broke out on his face.

"Geordi!" he exclaimed. "Captain!" He held out a hand to them.

Being a bit closer, Geordi was the first to take it.

"It's good to see you, Data."

Picard shook hands with him, too.

"It's been a long time," he noted.

The android nodded. "Too long, sir." Turning to his housekeeper, he said, "Jessel, these are my old shipmates. The ones I have told you about."

The woman harrumphed. "Oh. The *Enterprise* bunch. How delightful." And turning on her heel, she vanished into the house.

Unperturbed, Data ushered them in. "What a pleasant surprise this is." And then, glancing back at the departing housekeeper: "Tea and biscuits for everyone, Jessel."

CHAPTER **6**

To Picard, Data's library looked like something out of a Sherlock Holmes story . . . spacious, comfortable, the walls lined with a wide assortment of leather-bound books. He could smell the oils that had been used to preserve them. A fire—not a real one, of course, but a rather authentic-looking hologram—was roaring cheerfully in the hearth.

And there were any number of cats wandering about or sleeping on the furniture. Apparently, the android's mixed experience with Spot hadn't turned him off to felines altogether.

La Forge nodded appreciatively. "This is quite a house you have here, Data. I see they treat professors pretty well at Cambridge."

The android shrugged. "Holding the Lucasian Chair does have its perquisites. This house originally belonged to Sir Isaac Newton when he held the position. It has since become the traditional residence." He paused. "Of course, being a creature of habit, I tend to use only three of the forty-seven rooms in the manor."

Just then, Jessel entered the room with a silver tea service, which gleamed in the firelight. Judging by her expression, she'd been keeping track of their conversation.

"Might as well board up the rest of the house, for all the use it gets . . ." Her voice trailed off, but she'd made her point.

Wiping her hands on her apron, she leaned in close to La Forge and spoke quietly—though not so quietly Picard couldn't make out what she was saying. "You're his friend, eh?"

He saw the former engineer nod. "That's right. And I have been for quite some time."

"Well then," said the housekeeper, "as his friend, see if you can get him to take that gray streak out of his hair. He looks like a bloomin' skunk, he does. People will soon start walking on the other side of the street when they see him coming."

Data, who had obviously overheard, cast a remonstrative look at Jessel. "Thank you," he told her. "That will be all."

Without another word, she made her exit. The android turned to his guests with a wry look on his face.

"She can be trying at times," he admitted. "But she does make me laugh now and then."

La Forge smiled. "So . . . what is it with your hair, anyway?"

Picard was glad someone else had mentioned it. Unfortunately, Data looked a bit embarrassed.

"I have found that a touch of gray adds an air

of . . . distinction," he explained. "Unfortunately, I don't seem to have it quite right yet." Indicating a pair of chairs, he glanced at each of his old comrades in turn. "Please," he said. "Make yourselves comfortable."

Crossing to the tea set, the android began to pour. When he was done, he brought them their cups.

Then, sitting down himself, he eyed Picard. "Since neither of you has a predilection for sudden visits, I assume you are not here just for afternoon tea."

Picard nodded, grateful for the opening. "That's true. Data, I need your help. . . ."

It took a while for him to explain what had happened to him—even longer than it should have, perhaps, thanks to his illness. But in the end, he managed to get it all out.

"I know how it sounds," the older man finished. "But it happened. It was real. I was back on the *Enterprise.*"

He saw Data and La Forge exchange a look—but he was willing to disregard it. After all, he told himself, if their positions and his were reversed, he would have been a bit skeptical as well.

"Temporal displacement would normally leave a residual tachyon signature," the android noted, as a dark brown cat walked over his lap. "I've scanned you, sir, but I can't see anything out of the ordinary." Turning to La Forge, he asked, "When this happened, did you notice anything unusual?"

The man with the artificial eyes shook his head. "No. We were walking through the vineyard and he just . . . stumbled."

Data considered that for a moment. He looked back to Picard. "And you say this happened to you twice?"

The older man nodded. "Twice that I *know* of . . . though I suppose it could've been more often. . . ." He hated not being able to remember. "I wish I could be more specific," he said, "but this damned condition of mine . . . I just can't seem to think straight sometimes."

At that point, Jessel entered to reclaim the tea service. By then, whatever they hadn't finished had gone cold— as a number of cats could bear witness, having peeked inside the cups themselves. While the housekeeper gathered up the cups and saucers, the android renewed his questioning.

"Captain," he began, "when was the last time you saw a physician about your Irumodic syndrome?"

Picard felt his spine stiffen. "A week ago. I was prescribed peridaxon. And yes, I'm fully aware that it's not a cure. Nothing can stop the deterioration of my . . . my synaptic pathways. I know that."

Again, Data and La Forge exchanged looks. This time, it rankled the older man, and he couldn't contain it.

"You think I'm senile," he told them. "That this is all some . . . delusion or something. Admit it."

"No one said anything like that," replied La Forge.

But Data gave him the unvarnished truth. "In all honesty, Captain, it's a thought that has occurred to me. However, there is nothing to disprove what you are saying, either. So I suppose it's possible that something *is* happening to you."

Picard felt hopeful as he watched the android pace across the room, sending a number of sleeping cats scurrying for cover. It seemed Data had become a lot more . . . *human* since they saw each other last. Or at least, he'd picked up some human habits.

"The first thing we should do," said their host, "is give you a complete series of neurographic scans. We can use the equipment at the biometrics lab here on campus." Turning to the housekeeper, who was shooing a Siamese cat off the couch, he said, "Jessel, ask Professor Rippert to take over my lecture for tomorrow . . . and possibly for the rest of the week."

The older man grinned. "That's my Data!" he exclaimed. "I knew I could count on you!" He jumped up from his chair and—

—felt his feet strike the unyielding metal of the shuttledeck.

Looking around, Picard had that feeling again . . . the one that he had been somewhere else until this very second. He was tempted to reach back, to steady himself against the *Galileo*. But in the next moment, the feeling passed.

A moment later, he saw that there were a couple of dozen officers lined up for his inspection. They were standing at ease in three distinct ranks.

One was a Klingon—Worf, wasn't it? He recalled the gist of the man's personal history. Nor was it a difficult task, considering how unusual it was for a Klingon to be raised on Earth.

Stepping out from behind Picard, Lieutenant Yar called out in a loud voice, "The commanding officer of the *Enterprise!*"

The words echoed from bulkhead to bulkhead. It was a proud moment for him. And it wasn't over. Right on cue, an ensign brought an old-fashioned bosun's whistle to his lips and blew on it. At the high, shrill sound, everyone in the bay snapped to crisp attention.

Shrugging off the last shreds of his disorientation, Picard moved to a nearby podium, placed his padd on it, and surveyed the crowd. There were other faces here that he recognized from their Starfleet files—but there would be time to study them at length later on. Right now, everyone was waiting for him to officially announce his assumption of command.

Moving forward with the ceremony, he read from the padd. "To Captain Jean-Luc Picard, stardate four-one-one-four-eight . . ."

Something made him look up. To his astonishment, there was a trio of humans up on the shuttle-bay's catwalk. They were haggard, sunken-cheeked . . . dressed in rags.

And the captain had the strangest feeling that he had seen them somewhere before—though he couldn't remember where.

As Picard stared at them, and they stared back, one of the figures pointed to him. Then all three began to laugh. The captain blinked, unable to believe the evidence of his own eyes.

And then they were gone.

Jarred, he just stood there for a moment, trying to decide what had just happened—if anything. He was a perfectly sane, perfectly rational human being. He had no history of hallucinations. And yet, he had thought he'd seen something that was plainly not there.

Someone cleared his or her throat. Remembering the officers who had assembled to greet him, Picard looked at them. They were waiting.

Gathering himself, he returned to the orders written on the padd. "You are hereby requested and required to take command . . ." he read.

And a second time, something caught his eye. Glancing up, he saw that the figures on the catwalk were back—but now, there were *six* of them. And they were pointing at him and jeering even more wildly than before.

Then, as if by magic, they weren't. They had vanished again. He looked all around the room and could find no sign of them.

It was only then that he put two and two together. Might the sight of the hollow-cheeked hecklers have something to do with his feelings of disorientation? Might it not be all of a piece?

Unfortunately, he couldn't puzzle it out now, in the presence of all his officers. They would think he'd gone over the edge.

Later, after he'd had time to rest, to mull it over, he'd be able to put these things in some reasonable context. He'd see that there was a logical explanation for all of it.

But right now, he wanted to get this ceremony over with and retire to his quarters. As before, he applied himself to reading the words on the padd.

". . . to take command of the *U.S.S. Enterprise* as of this date. Signed, Rear Admiral Norah Satie, Starfleet Command."

Turning off the padd, he stepped out from behind the podium and looked at his crew. They looked back at him silently, waiting for the first words he would offer them—their first bit of sage advice from the captain of the newly commissioned *Enterprise.*

But before he could advise them, he saw that the scraggly figures had returned—and this time, in force. There were ten of them now, up on the catwalk, all shouting at Picard with murderous intent. Out of reflex, he took a step back, prepared to respond if they came leaping over the rail to get at him.

But it never happened—because a fraction of a second later, they were gone. An eerie, echoing silence filled the shuttlebay, as the captain made his decision.

This wasn't his imagination. This wasn't the product of a tired or distracted mind. Something was going on here—and until he knew what, he would take whatever precautions he deemed necessary.

Addressing his officers, he shouted, "Red alert! All hands to battle stations!"

For a moment, they just looked at him, dumbfounded. Surely, their faces said, this had to be a joke. Only one of them took it seriously right from the start.

"You heard the captain!" barked Lieutenant Yar. "Move!"

That broke them out of their initial paralysis. An instant later, they were sounding the alert, rushing out the shuttlebay doors to their respective duty stations.

And as Picard watched them go, he mused that in twenty years on the *Stargazer,* he had never encountered *anything* like this. Welcome to the *Enterprise,* he told himself.

CHAPTER 7

"Red alert," muttered Miles Edward O'Brien, lost in thought as he made his way along the crowded corridor. "I just don't get it."

His friend Sutcliffe, who was accompanying him to the turbolift, didn't get it either. He said so.

"I mean," he continued, "I've heard of captains coming on board and trying to make an impression, but that was ridiculous. Everybody running to their battle stations for no reason at all . . ." He sighed. "If it was a drill, it was a damned stupid time for one."

O'Brien cast a sideways glance at him. "Don't say that."

Sutcliffe glanced back. "Say what?"

"That it was stupid," O'Brien explained.

"And why not?" asked the other man.

"Because he's the captain," O'Brien told him.

"And that means he can't do anything stupid?"

O'Brien nodded. "That's right."

"You're out of your mind," said Sutcliffe. "Captains are as human as anyone else. Or as Vulcan. Or as Andorian. They make mistakes, just like the rest of us."

"That's not the way *I* was taught," O'Brien countered. "You don't run down the man in the center seat. Not even when you're talking to a friend. Not even when you're talking to *yourself.*" He paused, remembering his old ship and its commanding officer. "That's the way it was on the *Phoenix,* under Captain Maxwell. And that's the way it'll be here—at least for *me.*"

Sutcliffe smiled. "Blind obedience? Really?"

O'Brien shrugged off the criticism. "Not blind," he said. "Just obedience. You may disagree with a man's orders, or his judgment. But when you start thinking you can replace it with your own, you run into trouble." He grunted. "Starfleet Command isn't in the habit of putting berserkers or ne'er-do-wells in charge of Galaxy-class vessels. If Captain Picard called a red alert, he had a reason for it."

"Uh-huh," Sutcliffe replied. "Even if you can't for the life of you imagine what it might have been."

O'Brien frowned. "Even then. Of course—"

Abruptly, he felt his shoulder bump hard into something. Or more accurately, someone. In this case, it was an Oriental woman with her arms full of transparent flower cases—which went tumbling to the deck as he and she collided.

"Oh, blast," he said, kneeling beside her to help her pick them up again. But she didn't seem to be in any hurry to do that.

"The *b'lednaya . . ."* she groaned, her dark eyes wide with pain.

"Don't worry," O'Brien told her. He smiled, trying to put the situation in perspective for her. "I'll give you a hand."

The woman looked up at him. "Don't bother," she said. *"B'lednaya* are very fragile. As you can see," she said, picking up a case to use as an example, "their stems have been broken."

Indeed, their stems *were* broken. And though the delicate, violet-and-yellow flowers hadn't been affected yet, it was only a matter of time before they'd begin to shrivel.

He felt badly about that. But he still had to get to the bridge to help with its outfitting, and he was due there in just a couple of minutes. Nor did he want to be tardy, considering the importance of his assignment.

Starfleet captains might understand a lot of things, but lateness wasn't one of them. He knew that from sad experience.

"Listen," he told the woman—who, he couldn't help but notice, was quite attractive—"I'm sorry, really I am. But I've got to make my shift. Are you sure I can't help you in some way?"

She couldn't have given him an icier stare if she'd been an ammonia-breather. "That's all right," she assured him. "I think you've helped enough . . . don't you?"

Well, thought O'Brien. If that's the way it was to be . . .

Straightening, he resumed his progress toward the turbolift. Sutcliffe, who was still beside him, clapped him on the shoulder.

"That's all right," he commented. "She wasn't your type anyway, Miles. Too delicate."

O'Brien glanced back over his shoulder at the woman. As she gathered up the cases full of ruined flowers, he felt a pang he'd never felt before. Guilt, probably. Or was it something else?

"You're probably right," he told Sutcliffe. But he still glanced back at her a couple more times before he reached his destination.

Tasha Yar didn't feel particularly comfortable in the Ten-Forward lounge. However, it had been one of the first areas in the ship to be completely furnished, and that made it perfect for the various meetings she had to conduct with the ship's personnel.

After all, she was one of the ranking officers on board. When the rest of the senior staff arrived, her responsibilities would be confined to security per se—but for now, it fell to her to coordinate everything from shuttledeck operations to outfitting sickbay.

At this particular moment, as she nursed her too-rich Dagavarian maltmilk, she was waiting to conduct a meeting with the latest shipment of shuttle pilots. She reeled off their names from memory: Collins, Mayhew, and Prieto. All highly rated, though none higher than her.

Tasha couldn't help but notice that everyone else in the lounge was seated in twos and threes. She was the only one sitting alone. But then, she was used to that. Coming from the kind of place *she'd* come from, it was unlikely that social interaction would ever be her forte.

Then she realized that there *was* one other singleton among all the tables in Ten-Forward. It was Counselor

Troi, who'd come aboard shortly after the security chief herself. And the Betazoid was looking at her.

A moment later, Troi turned away. But it was too late. Tasha had noticed the scrutiny. And being the kind of person she was, she decided to do something about it.

Picking up her maltmilk, she approached the counselor's table. And without waiting for an invitation, she sat down. Troi smiled, though not without a bit of curiosity in her eyes.

Tasha didn't believe in casual conversation. "You were staring at me," she observed. "Don't deny it."

The Betazoid's smile faded. "Yes," she admitted after a moment. "I suppose I was."

Her honesty surprised the security chief. But it didn't make her bristle any the less. "Because you find my case intriguing," she suggested. "Or maybe just because you had nothing better to do."

Troi's brows came together above her perfectly shaped nose. "I beg your pardon, Lieutenant?"

Tasha grunted. "So what do you think?" she asked. "How does my childhood on Turkana Four stack up with some of the other personal histories you've had the pleasure of dissecting?"

She felt herself stiffen as the memories flooded her. None of them were good.

"I mean," she continued, "do most of your patients see their parents killed in a cadre crossfire at the age of five? Do they spend their lives sleeping in cold, wet tunnels—or rather, never sleeping, because they've always got to keep an ear out for cadre foragers?"

The counselor shook her head. "Lieutenant . . . Tasha . . . I—"

"I know," said the security chief. "You're a professional. You're not the least bit shocked about the things I had to do in order to survive. About the blood I had to spill. About the lies I had to tell, or the alliances I had to forge, or the . . . compromises I had to make in order to get off that festering wound of a world."

Troi frowned. "I am sorry," she said, "but I don't know what you're talking about. Or at least, I didn't— until now."

Tasha looked at her. The counselor seemed sincere, and yet . . . "You're a Betazoid, aren't you? You read minds," she declared, her tone one of accusation.

"Actually," Troi explained, "I'm only half-Betazoid. My father was human. As a result, I can only sense emotional states." She paused. "Growing up a non-telepath on Betazed was a distinct disadvantage— though nothing like what you've experienced, apparently."

The lieutenant felt her cheeks turning hot with embarrassment. "You can't read my mind?" she said. "Then why were you staring at me just now?"

The counselor looked apologetic. "I know," she admitted. "That was rude. It's just that I was wondering about you. I mean, I knew a little from your personnel file, but there was a lot I didn't know. And it's my job to develop an understanding of every officer on this ship."

Tasha sat back in her chair. "Then you weren't prying into my mind? You weren't reading my thoughts?"

Troi shook her head. "Even if I could, I wouldn't. As much as I need to understand you, I can't go delving into your psyche without your permission. It wouldn't be ethical."

The security chief looked at her. She felt absolutely ... stupid. "It seems an apology is in order, Counselor —but from me to you, rather than the other way around."

Troi shook her head. "That is not necessary. You made a mistake—and not even a big one. I am willing to forget it if you are."

Tasha smiled. "Done." As she gazed across the table at the Betazoid ... or rather, half-Betazoid ... she hoped that someday they might become friends. That would be nice, considering the fact that they were both senior staff members, and would likely be working closely together for a long time to come.

Also, it was good to know that there was someone on this ship she could depend on—someone she could call on in a crisis. Given the captain's already apparent idiosyncrasies, she wasn't sure she would want to call on *him.*

Suddenly, Troi's eyes opened wide, as she saw something over Tasha's shoulder. "My god," she said. "Look out!"

The security chief had always been proud of her reflexes. In one fluid motion, she rose from her chair and whirled—in time to see the waiter stumbling in her direction with a tray loaded with hot drinks.

Someone else would have been lucky to elude the drinks as they spilled. Tasha was able to catch the waiter and steady the tray, so that only a little of the hot liquid washed over onto the lounge's soft deck covering.

"Sorry," said the waiter, looking stricken in the face of his clumsiness. "Are you all right?" he asked.

The lieutenant scowled. "Try to be a little more

careful next time. The counselor and I could've wound
up in sickbay with some nice burns."

"I know," the waiter agreed. "It's just that we're
running all over the place, trying to keep everyone
happy. They need someone to take charge of this place.
Someone who knows what he's doing."

Tasha looked at him. "Or *she,*" she suggested.

The waiter sighed. "Or *she.* Just as long as they get
someone."

As he retreated, heeding the lieutenant's advice to be
more careful, Troi shook her head ruefully. "You know,"
she commented, "I helped design this place."

Tasha turned to her. "Did you?"

The counselor nodded as the security chief sat down.
"The idea was to have a venue where people could let off
a little steam. Resolve conflicts. Make new friends.
Thirty years from now, when I've retired to do something else, I envision this place continuing to do my
work for me."

"You just didn't take into account the need for a
strong manager," observed Tasha.

Troi made a sound of resignation. "Apparently. But
then, lounge management wasn't exactly my specialty."

As the security chief smiled, unable to help herself, she
remembered her meeting. "Excuse me," she said. "I'm
supposed to get together with some new shuttle pilots.
You know, to get them acclimated to the way we do
things here."

"I understand," the counselor assured her. "But stay
here. I have to go now, anyway . . . you can have the
table all to yourself."

As she rose, not even waiting for a response, her expression changed. It became a little more serious.

"And, Tasha . . . if you ever feel you need someone to talk to . . ."

"I'll know where to look," said the lieutenant sincerely. "Thanks. I mean it."

With that, Troi headed for the exit. As Tasha watched her go, she saw a couple of the shuttle pilots meander in. Collins and Mayhew were just a little early, she noted. But where was Prieto?

Catching sight of her, Mayhew pointed in her direction, and both pilots crossed the lounge to join her. As they sat down, they seemed eager to hear what she had to say. And why not? The sooner they were briefed, the sooner they could do what they were trained to do: fly shuttles.

"Where's your friend?" she asked them. "Prieto?"

They glanced at each other. "Er . . . actually . . ." Collins began.

"He said he'd meet us here," supplied Mayhew. "As soon as he was . . ."

Tasha looked at him. "Yes?"

Mayhew winced. "He had a previous engagement, Lieutenant."

She grunted. "I see. A romantic liaison, you mean?"

The pilot looked as if he were barefooting it over hot coals. "Something like that."

Tasha glanced at the chronometer on the wall—a temporary fixture, as she understood it. Something about people not being able to relax if they were too aware of the time.

"By my reckoning," she said, "Prieto's got exactly

thirty-nine seconds to show up. And if he doesn't, he'll be old and gray before he—"

Abruptly, the doors to Ten-Forward slid aside and Prieto came bounding in. Without ceremony, he pulled up a chair and sat down between his fellow pilots.

"Sorry I cut it so close," he said. "You see, I—"

"Save it," Tasha told him. She scowled. "Honestly, Prieto. It's guys like you that'll be the death of me."

Picard's quarters weren't quite set up yet. In fact, they were hardly set up at all. There were only a monitor and a couple of pieces of furniture in the anteroom.

Still, it was a shelter—a haven from the wondering glances of his crew, who were no doubt still puzzled by his call to battle stations. Truth to tell, he was puzzled himself—not by the action itself, of course, but by the circumstances that had prompted it.

He had pretty much concluded that his spells of disorientation and the strangers who had appeared on the shuttledeck were all part of some larger problem. He just couldn't imagine what it could be.

Unexpectedly, there was a sound of chimes. The door, thought the captain. But who would be calling on him?

"Come," he said.

As the doors opened, they revealed a round, blue-skinned Bolian in civilian garb. The Bolian smiled, perhaps a little too graciously.

"My name is Mot," he announced. "I will be one of your barbers."

Picard stared at him. There had been no barbers on the *Stargazer*. There simply hadn't been room for them.

But on the *Enterprise,* it seemed, with its considerable population, there was room for almost everything.

Including raggedy wraiths who taunted him from the catwalk.

"Pleased to meet you, Mot," said the captain.

In point of fact, he much preferred to be alone right now. There was too much to sort out, and he had a feeling it was important to do it sooner rather than later.

"Pleased to meet *you,* sir," replied the Bolian. "Of course, I would rather be speaking to you as you sat in my chair, particularly as I can see that you're in need of some attention . . . but like your quarters, the barbershop is not yet fully equipped."

Picard nodded in what he hoped looked like sympathy. "I'm sure that problem will be rectified at the earliest opportunity," he remarked. "The outfitting of your shop, I mean."

"I hope so," Mot went on. "You see, a barbershop is a most essential facility on a vessel of this size. It is a place where ideas are exchanged . . . where consensuses are reached . . . where the social fabric is woven and rewoven. And, of course, where hair is cut with the utmost delicacy and artfulness."

The captain had a feeling that this conversation would go on for hours, if he wasn't careful. Perhaps days.

"I see what you mean," he said. "I'll tell you what. As soon as we've finished our visit, I'll speak with the officer in charge of your deck—and he or she will see to it that the barbershop becomes a top priority."

The Bolian looked delighted. "How kind of you," he remarked. "I hope I will have an opportunity to repay your kindness." He looked at Picard with a critical eye. "In fact, I could go and get my instruments right now. I normally don't make appointments in quarters, but for someone like yourself . . . whose last barber was obviously lacking in technique . . ."

"No," said the captain, a bit too quickly. "That will not be necessary . . . really."

Mot seemed not to have taken offense. "I understand. You wish to wait until I can accommodate you in the shop. You prefer to participate in the complete experience, to bask in the glow of tradition."

"Yes," Picard responded, becoming a little exasperated. "That's it. That's it exactly. Now, if you don't mind, I—"

"I might have known you'd be a purist," observed the Bolian, "coming from a long line of vintners as you do. Well, you'll be glad to know that barbering has been in my family for generations . . . almost as long as winemaking has been in yours."

Something flashed through the captain's mind, though he couldn't quite catch it. "How . . . how do you know so much about my background?" he asked. He was legitimately curious.

"I'm a barber," Mot said proudly—as if that explained it all. "And as I was saying, I come by it honestly. As you Picards toiled in your Terran vineyards, we honed our shears in our shops on Bol. In fact . . ."

The captain was no longer listening. At the moment when Mot mentioned the Picard family vineyards, that same something had flashed through his mind again. But this time, it lingered as a dreamlike image.

Of a misty sunrise. Of a vine that needed tying. And of a visit from an old friend, with eyes that weren't quite right.

But in the dream—if it *was* a dream—the captain's hands were old and stiff and difficult to work with. And his mind wasn't quite as sharp. And his visitor was . . .

. . . was *Geordi*. He remembered now—not just the vineyard, but everything. It came flooding into his brain, a river in springtime overflowing its dam.

That vineyard . . . those gnarled and knobby fingers . . . existed in the future. In *his* future—or some latter stage of it, because he had memories of a different stage as well.

Picard gasped as something else struck him. The haggard figures he'd seen on the shuttledeck . . . he'd seen them in the vineyard as well. Of a certainty, he had.

Perhaps there had been fewer of them, but they'd been there just the same—pointing and deriding him as they had just a little while ago. And like the officers assembled on the shuttledeck, the Geordi of the future had seen neither hide nor hair of them.

Only the captain could see them. But why? Who or what could be responsible for such a . . . ?

And then he knew. Or at least, he was able to guess . . . because now his knowledge extended over the thirty-two years that hadn't happened yet.

"Of course," the Bolian droned on, oblivious of Picard's cogitations, "I remained in the business, as my father wished. But I respect you just as much for striking out on your own. Really, I do. It's not every—"

"Mr. Mot," the captain interrupted. "I don't mean to be curt, but there's a great deal for me to attend to. I would appreciate it if we could continue this conversation at some other time."

The Bolian looked at him. "Oh. Certainly we can." He smiled again in that too-gracious way of his. "And the shop . . . ?"

"Special attention," Picard promised.

Though he would not have thought it possible, Mot's smile actually broadened. "In that case, I'll take my leave of you," he told the captain. "As you'll no doubt understand, I have a great deal to attend to as well."

Picard couldn't imagine what that might be, but he nodded knowingly—and watched the Bolian back out through the doors with a last, parting wave.

"Thank you," called the barber, as the doors closed again.

"No," said the captain, mostly to himself. "Thank *you.*"

CHAPTER 8

Captain's personal log: stardate 41153.7. Recorded under security lockout Omega three-two-seven. I am now convinced that I am shifting between three different time periods in my life. I've also decided not to inform this crew of my experiences. If it's true that I've traveled to the past, I cannot risk giving them advance knowledge of what's to come.

Picard stared out one of the ports in the *Enterprise*'s observation lounge as three of his officers filed into the room behind him. Later on, they were to pick up additional personnel at a nearby starbase. But for now, he would make do with Lieutenant Yar, Counselor Troi, and Lieutenant Worf.

Knowing that none of them would sit before he did, the captain took a seat at the head of the polished, synthetic-wood table. A moment later, the others followed suit.

In the future, Picard would come to know these people well. He would come to trust them implicitly. For the time being, however, he eyed them warily, and they looked at him the same way. At this point, they were comfortable neither with him nor with one another.

Addressing Yar, he said, "Report, Lieutenant."

She wasn't at all taken aback by his curtness. In fact, he thought, she seemed to prefer it.

"We've completed a full subspace scan of the ship and surrounding space," said Yar. "We detected no unusual readings or anomalies."

The Klingon spoke up. "With all due respect, sir . . . it would help if we knew what we were looking for."

The captain nodded. "Your comment is noted, Mr. Worf." He turned to the Betazoid—or more accurately, half-Betazoid, since her father had been human. "Counselor, do you sense anything unusual aboard the *Enterprise* . . . say, an alien presence that doesn't belong here . . . perhaps operating on a level of intelligence superior to our own?"

Troi applied her empathic powers. A little while later, she shook her head. "No, sir. I'm only aware of the crew . . . and the families aboard the ship, of course."

"I see," said Picard. Getting up, he took a few steps around the table. He knew that their eyes were on him—that they were sizing him up even as they awaited his orders. "Mr. Worf, I want you to initiate a level-two security alert on all decks until further notice."

The Klingon looked surprised. As the captain watched, Worf glanced at Yar, an awkward expression on his face. The blond woman stood and met Picard's gaze. Clearly, she was perturbed.

"Sir, with all due respect . . . *I'm* the security chief on this ship. Unless you're planning to make a change, that is . . ."

The captain cursed inwardly. She was right, of course. It was just that his instinct was to think of *Worf* as the security chief.

"No," he assured her. "I'm planning no such thing. Security alert two, Lieutenant."

Yar inclined her head slightly. "Aye, sir."

But before she could move to comply, they heard a voice piped in over the ship's intercom system: "Captain Picard to the bridge, please."

Picard knew the voice. It belonged to O'Brien—to whom he'd assigned primary conn duties.

"On my way, Chief," he informed O'Brien. Then, leading the others out of the lounge, he exited onto the bridge.

As Tasha followed her new captain out of the observation lounge, she saw Miles O'Brien, a rather likable Irishman, waiting for them in the command area with a padd in his hand. As Picard approached, O'Brien extended it to him.

All around them, crew members were busy at one task or another—hooking up the circuitry in an open panel, lugging diagnostic equipment around, or linking a console to the ship's computer. It was chaos—but no different from what one would expect on a vessel still being outfitted for duty.

"What's this?" the captain asked O'Brien over the clamor.

The chief grunted. "Starfleet has just issued an alert, sir. It appears a number of vessels are moving toward the Neutral Zone between Romulan and Federation space."

That caught Tasha's interest. "What kind of vessels?" she asked.

O'Brien turned to her. "Freighters, transports . . . all civilian. None of them Federation ships."

As Picard read the specifics on the padd, he frowned. Tasha got the impression that it meant something almost . . . personal to him.

"It says," he announced, "that a large spatial anomaly has appeared in the Neutral Zone. In the Devron system."

Worf's response was quick and heated—no surprise, given his racial heritage. The Klingons and the Romulans, once allies, were now the most vicious of enemies.

"Perhaps it is a Romulan trick," he suggested. "A plan to lure ships into the Neutral Zone as an excuse for a military strike."

O'Brien eyed the Klingon. "I don't know about that, sir. But Starfleet's canceling our mission to Farpoint Station and ordering us to the Neutral Zone as soon as we can leave spacedock."

To Tasha, that news wasn't all bad. Sitting here in drydock had made her edgy—irritable. She couldn't wait to put this new ship of theirs through its paces, and as far as she was concerned, the Neutral Zone was as good a place to do that as any.

"No," said the captain.

She looked at him, a little taken aback. *"No,* sir?"

"That's correct," he told her. "We will *not* go to the Neutral Zone. We will proceed to Farpoint, as planned."

Tasha looked at him. She began to object—but Worf beat her to it.

"Captain," he blurted, "the security of the Federation may be at stake! How can we—"

Picard silenced him with a glance. "Man your station, Mr. Worf—or I will find someone who can."

For an instant, Tasha didn't know whether the Klingon would back down or not. But a moment later, he whirled angrily and returned to the aft science station that he had been working on.

Troi frowned. "Captain, perhaps if we understood your thinking . . . if you could explain . . ."

Unflappable, Picard shook his head. "I don't intend to explain anything, Counselor . . ." Then he turned to Tasha, as if she represented the rest of the crew. "To anyone," he said, completing his sentence. "We will proceed to Farpoint Station, as I indicated."

For what seemed like a long time, nobody moved. There was an air of quiet tension on the bridge that nobody seemed eager to break.

Tasha tried to come to grips with the captain's intransigence. Surely, he could see that a confrontation with the Romulans—even a *potential* confrontation—wasn't something to be ignored. And their mission at Farpoint was hardly an urgent one.

Now that she thought about it, Picard had been acting strangely almost since she met him. First, she'd caught him staring at her on the shuttle. Then, in the shuttle-bay, he'd given the red-alert order even when there was no imminent danger. And finally, in the observation lounge, he'd forgotten that she was chief of security.

She'd chalked up his staring to some distraction connected with his new assignment. The red-alert order . . . well, at the time, she'd imagined he just wanted to keep them on their toes. And as much as she'd resented the mix-up in protocol, it seemed like an honest mistake —if one that a top-notch officer could be expected to avoid.

Now, however, there was *this.* A directive to disregard Starfleet orders. An option within the captain's purview, to be sure—but one that was rarely exercised, and only after careful consideration.

Picard turned to O'Brien. "Now, if I'm not mistaken, Chief, we're having some problems with the warp plasma inducers."

O'Brien seemed surprised. "That's right, sir. But how did . . ."

"I think I know a way to get them back on-line," the captain continued. "You're with me, Chief." To Tasha, he said, "We'll be in main engineering if you need one of us."

She nodded and watched the two of them exit into the turbolift. No sooner were they gone than she saw Worf make his way toward her. He came close enough to keep anyone else from hearing what he was saying.

"I do not understand," muttered the Klingon. "The Romulans may be planning an attack, and he does not seem to care." A pause. "Are you certain this is the same man who commanded the *Stargazer?* Who defeated the Ferengi at Maxia Zeta?"

Tasha shrugged. "As far as I know," she replied.

He grunted. "What are you going to do?"

Indeed, what *would* she do? Alert Starfleet to Picard's contrary ways? Or follow the instructions he had laid out for them?

"I'm going to do what I'm told," she answered finally. "And prepare to go to Farpoint."

That was obviously not the response Worf wanted to hear. Still, it was the only one she was prepared to make . . . for *now.*

Picard sat in the chief engineer's office, at a console, with Miles O'Brien standing beside him. Out in main engineering, in the shadow of the warp reactor, several crewmen were getting the ship ready to go.

But what the captain was doing was even more essential—a job that would have taken many hours, under normal circumstances. Fortunately, he *remembered* what the problem was—and knew how to take care of it. That was one advantage of having lived in the future.

Handing O'Brien a padd, the captain sat back in his chair. He watched for a moment as the redheaded man looked it over.

"I've bypassed the secondary plasma inducer," Picard explained. "Now I want to begin realigning the power grid to the specifications I've given you. Any questions?"

O'Brien's eyes narrowed as he pondered what the captain was calling for. When he looked up again, there was a certain amount of insecurity in his expression.

"You have to realize, sir . . . this isn't exactly my area

of expertise. The chief engineer should be making these modifications."

"But the chief engineer isn't on board yet," Picard pointed out. "Nor will she be for some time. And even if she were, I asked *you* to do the job."

O'Brien still looked less than confident. He seemed to need a boost of some sort.

Leaning back in his chair, the captain added, "Chief . . . trust me. I *know* you can do this. All those years you spent as a child building model starship engines represented time well spent."

O'Brien stared at him as if Picard had just confessed to being a Ferengi on his mother's side. "How did you know *that,* sir?"

Abruptly, the captain realized that he'd put his foot in his mouth. O'Brien had confided that information to him, he remembered now . . . but in a conversation that wouldn't take place until years hence.

Picard cleared his throat to cover his reaction. "From . . . your Starfleet records, of course. Where else could I have learned such a thing?"

The other man looked impressed. "Really, sir? I didn't think anyone studied those things so closely."

"Really," said the captain, relieved that O'Brien seemed to believe him. He would have to be more careful about such things if he was to accomplish anything in this time period. "Now, about that power grid . . ."

O'Brien smiled. Apparently, he felt a bit more equal to the task, now that his ego had been massaged. "Yes, sir. I'll get right on it."

Taking the padd, he headed across the engineering section. Picard watched as the chief recruited several of the other crewmen on duty, taking them away from less important work.

"Fletcher," called O'Brien. "Tell Munoz and Lee to get up here right away. We have to realign the entire power grid. We're all going to be burning the midnight oil on this one."

"That would be inadvisable," came a reply from a part of engineering that the captain couldn't see. Getting up from what would be Geordi La Forge's desk in due time—though it would belong to several others before him—he walked over to the office door and peered around it.

"Ah," he said softly, understanding the remark now that he knew who had made it.

As he looked on, Commander Data approached O'Brien. From the looks of it, they were meeting for the first time.

"Excuse me?" replied the chief.

"If you attempt to ignite a petroleum product on this ship at zero-hundred hours," the android warned him, "it will activate the fire-suppression system, which will seal off this entire compartment."

Picard had forgotten how naive Data had been when he first arrived on the *Enterprise* . . . how innocent and literal. It was amazing how far he had come in the years since.

In the meantime, O'Brien seemed to be at a loss. "Sir," he ventured, "that was just an expression."

The android looked at him. "An expression of what?"

The redhead groped for a response. "Er . . . a figure of

speech, you know? I was trying to tell Mr. Fletcher here that . . . we were going to be working *late."*

Data tilted his head to the side as he absorbed the information. "I see," he replied at last. "Then to 'burn the midnight oil' implies late work?"

O'Brien smiled a little tentatively. "That's right."

"I am curious," said the android. "What is the etymology of that idiom? How did it come to be used in contemporary language?"

The chief recoiled a bit at that one. "I don't believe I know, sir. If you like, I suppose I could . . ."

Finally, the captain came to O'Brien's rescue. "Commander Data," he enthused, "welcome aboard. It's good to see you."

And it was. Picard smiled at him warmly, genuinely glad to have someone here he could completely rely on.

The android turned and acknowledged the captain's presence. No doubt, thought Picard, he didn't comprehend why this man he had just met was being so friendly to him. But, like a lot of things, he seemed to take it in stride.

"It is . . . reasonably good to see you, too, sir," Data replied.

The captain indicated a wall panel near the warp core with a tilt of his head. "I could use your assistance with the infusor array. There are a few adjustments I'd like to make."

Data's head moved ever so slightly. "Certainly," he said.

Together, they moved to the wall panel and pried it open. Picard pointed to a conduit.

"As you can see, we're having a bit of difficulty here.

Something seems not to be working very well, though we've been unable to determine what it is . . ."

The android scrutinized the mechanism behind the panel. "This will require a completely new field induction subprocessor," he concluded. He turned to the captain. "It appears that we will be required to . . . ignite the midnight petroleum, sir."

Picard smiled. Data learned quickly, didn't he? Focusing his attention on the mechanism, the captain . . .

. . . found himself staring at a darkened monitor. Looking around, he saw that he was in Beverly's office, back in what he had come to think of as the "present." And as if to emphasize his lack of control over his existence, he was still in his bathrobe.

"Jean-Luc . . . what's going on?"

He turned to see Beverly herself standing at the entrance to the office. Riker was standing behind her, his eyes asking the same question that the doctor had asked out loud.

"It happened again," he told them.

Beverly's brow creased. "A time shift?"

He nodded. "Yes."

She held up a hand. "Don't move," she told him—and disappeared. A moment later, she came back with a medical tricorder and used it to scan Picard's head.

"What happened?" inquired Riker.

The captain sighed. "It's still a little vague . . . but I can remember more of it this time. I think the more often I shift between time periods, the more memory I retain." He stopped to gather his thoughts. "First, I was in what appeared to be the future . . . years from now. Then I was in the past again . . . right before our first mission."

Having finished her scan, Beverly read the results. Her eyes narrowed at something she saw there.

"What is it?" asked the first officer.

The doctor shook her head in disbelief. "I scanned his temporal lobe—and compared it with what I found just a few minutes ago. There's a *thirteen* percent increase in neurotransmitter activity in his hippocampus." She looked directly at Picard. "Within a matter of minutes, you accumulated over *two days'* worth of memories."

"Two days?" repeated Riker. "But that's . . ."

"Impossible?" Picard suggested. He nodded. "Unless you've spent a lot of time somewhere else between ticks of the clock."

He smiled grimly. Finally, they had some *proof* of what he was experiencing. He wasn't crazy—he was *actually* traveling through time.

CHAPTER 9

The *habak* was a rectangular room in a high tower, which served the Indians of Darvon V as a ceremonial chamber. The only way to enter it was via a wooden ladder that came through a hole in the floor. Another ladder led through a hole in the ceiling, which opened the place to the long, pale rays of the sun.

There was also a firepit. Though it hadn't been used for several days, it still gave off a thick, acrid smell of burned wood.

Wesley Crusher had spent the morning studying the sacred hangings that decorated the walls of the *habak.* He had studied them before; he would study them many more times before his journey—or this part of it—was done.

And the funny thing was, as many times as he scrutinized the woven wall hangings and the colorful symbols that populated them, he never grew bored. There always seemed to be some level of meaning he hadn't contemplated yet . . . some subtle, new wisdom to be discovered in them.

"Wesley?"

The young man turned and saw that the Traveler had joined him in the chamber. Wes hadn't seen him enter, but that was nothing unusual. The Traveler didn't come and go as normal people did.

More and more as time went on, neither did Wesley himself. As he practiced translating himself into other planes of existence, he was gradually eliminating the need to walk anywhere . . . or, in this case, to climb a ladder.

Of course, most of the time, he walked and climbed anyway. It just felt better. And a part of him hoped that it always would.

"Yes, Traveler?" he replied.

The being from Tau Ceti eyed him with an intensity that surprised him. "Do you not sense it?" he asked.

Sense . . . *it?* Wesley shook his head. "No . . . I don't. What is it I'm supposed to sense?"

Rather than answer out loud, the Traveler moved to one of the wall hangings and pointed. The young man followed his teacher's finger to a picture of something bright and multicolored—something Wesley couldn't readily identify. What's more, he was reasonably certain that the image hadn't been there before.

Opening his mind to it, he wove himself into the picture's reality—inspecting it not only on this plane, but on several others. He was intrigued to see how pervasive it was, how it seemed to transcend every layer of existence he touched.

Then, urged by an instinct he couldn't name or

pretend to understand, he turned to another image near it. This one was more easily recognizable. It was the *Enterprise*. But like the burst of color, he found, it existed on more than one plane.

Suddenly, Wesley got it. When he turned back to the Traveler, it was with a weight on his heart. "No," he said. "I can't let it happen."

"It is *already* happening," his teacher advised him.

"Then I've got to stop it," he said.

The Traveler smiled benignly at him. "Then you believe it is wise for you to intervene?"

The young man's mouth went dry as dust. "Traveler . . . they're my friends. My family. How can I *fail* to intervene?"

His teacher continued to smile. "Not so long ago, it appeared that there would be violence in this village. Do you remember?"

Wesley nodded. How could he forget? The Indians who lived here had made prisoners of some Cardassians, and Captain Picard had been duty-bound to free them. For a few tense moments, the Federation security team had squared off against the villagers, and it seemed like a good bet that there would be blood spilled before the day was out.

He had wanted to do something back then—but the Traveler had convinced him not to. He'd said, "They must find their own destinies, Wesley. It is not our place to interfere." And then: "Have faith in their abilities to solve their problems on their own."

Sure enough, the captain found a way to avoid disaster that day. But was it sheer luck that things had worked out . . . or did the Traveler know in advance that it would happen that way? Even after all his studies, Wesley still wasn't entirely sure.

"Is it like . . . the Prime Directive?" he asked out loud. "Are we forbidden to get involved?"

His teacher shrugged a bit. "There are always laws, Wesley. Some are self-imposed, and others are imposed upon us—but they are laws nonetheless."

The human frowned as he glanced again at the burst of color. "But aren't there times when a law needs to be broken? Aren't there exceptions?"

The Traveler tilted his head in a way that made him look a little like Data. "Perhaps. But to whom should we entrust that decision? Who has the wisdom to know when we should make an exception?"

Wesley sighed. It *was* like the Prime Directive. "Then I can't do a thing to help them? To tell them what's going on?"

His teacher gazed at him sympathetically. "If I were you," he replied finally, "I would not interfere . . . even if it were within my power."

The human walked over to the bench that was built into the western wall and sat down heavily. Running his fingers through his hair, he breathed a ragged breath.

"Mom . . ." he whispered.

Riker shook his head as he sat in his customary place at the observation lounge's dark, reflective table, surrounded by the ship's other senior officers. He'd seen his share of fantastic phenomena, but this one took the cake.

The idea that the captain was traveling through time, the victim of some capricious agency as yet beyond their understanding . . . it was bizarre, to say the least. And more than a little unsettling.

As the first officer gazed at Picard, he had the feeling that the captain might pop in and out of their reality at any time—an entire journey, perhaps two or three days' worth, completed in the space of an eyeblink.

Still, it wasn't anyone's imagination. It was *happening*. Dr. Crusher had shown him proof of that—and they'd had their run-ins with Time before, so they all knew that temporal travel was possible.

Riker might have felt better if they'd had a little more to go on—some data they could sink their collective teeth into. Unfortunately, they had nothing of the kind.

But then, that was the purpose of this meeting, wasn't it? To see what they could nail down with regard to Picard's time-shifting. And then to see what—if anything—they could do about it.

"Thank you all for being prompt," the captain told them. "As you know," he added only half-seriously, "time is of the essence." Then, turning to Deanna, he asked, "Counselor, do you remember the first day I came aboard the *Enterprise?*"

She returned his gaze. "Yes, I think I do."

Picard leaned forward. "What happened after the welcoming ceremony?"

"You mean after you disembarked from the *Galileo?*"

He nodded. "Yes."

Deanna thought for a moment. "There was a reception in Ten-Forward. I introduced you to Worf and the other senior officers. . . ."

The captain held up his hand to stop her. "Do you have any memory of me calling for a red alert in spacedock? Do you remember Starfleet diverting us from Farpoint to the Neutral Zone to investigate a spatial anomaly?"

She thought again. "No . . . I don't."

Picard leaned back in his chair. "As you may have gathered, I *do.* I experienced those events just a few short hours ago."

"It would appear," remarked Data, "that there is a discontinuity between the time periods you have described. Events in one period would seem to have no effect on the other two."

"And yet," Riker offered, "in both the past and the present . . . there's a report of the same anomaly in the Devron system. It's hard for me to believe that's a coincidence."

The captain nodded. "And for all I know, there may be a similar anomaly in the future, as well."

"Maybe," commented Geordi, "the anomaly is some kind of . . . temporal disruption." He positioned his hands as if he were holding a bowl, in an attempt to describe the thing. "A hole in the continuum, so to speak."

Beverly turned to Picard. "But how is all this related to your time-shifting?"

The captain grunted. "A good question. I suspect I may have some answers when I make my next round-trip to the past . . . or the future, whichever comes first."

"In the meantime," Riker reminded him, "we've got the Romulans to keep us from getting bored."

Picard turned to him, acknowledging the need for discussion. Regardless of what else was happening to him, that problem hadn't gone away.

"Thank you for reminding me, Number One. Insofar as the current mission is concerned, all departments should submit combat-readiness reports by oh-eight-hundred hours tomorrow." He looked from one face to the next. "I hope it won't come to that, of course—but if it does, I want to be ready. Dismissed."

Everyone rose to go, intent on their respective assignments. As Deanna headed for the door, Riker caught her attention.

"Looks like it's going to be a late night," he said. "Want to get some dinner first?"

There was something in her eyes that he hadn't quite expected. A hesitation, a feeling of awkwardness. He wondered why.

"Actually," said Deanna, "I . . ." She glanced over the first officer's shoulder. "I mean . . . *we* have plans."

Riker turned to follow her gaze—and found himself looking at Worf. It caught him off-guard, but he recovered quickly enough.

Apparently, the relationship between Deanna and his Klingon friend had progressed further than he realized. But hell . . . that was no fault of theirs, was it? They didn't have to keep the first officer apprised of their every move.

"I see," he said, doing his best to sound casual. "Well, then . . . see you tomorrow morning."

Worf inclined his massive head. "Good night, sir."

Riker inclined his head in turn. "Worf . . ."

He stood there for a moment, watching the two of them file out after the others—and acknowledged an emptiness in the pit of his belly that was directly related to the sight.

Not that he had any right to tell either of them whom they could spend their time with. No one was in a position to do *that.*

But, even though he and Deanna hadn't been lovers for several years now—since his assignment on Betazed came to an end—he'd always thought of her as his special friend. His confidante. His close companion.

And now, he saw that someone else might be taking his place in that regard. Someone he liked and respected, true—but it was still a change he wasn't looking forward to.

Or was there more to it than that? Did his feelings run deeper than he cared to admit? At some level, had he harbored the hope that, in the end, he and Deanna would wind up together again?

Beleaguered by such disturbing thoughts, he sighed and went back out onto the bridge.

CHAPTER 10

Picard paused by the aft science station to give Data his orders. The android's face was caught in the glare of his monitors.

"I want continuous subspace sweeps," he said. "We might detect a temporal disturbance."

"Aye, sir," replied Data. Without hesitation, he got to work manipulating his instruments.

Seeing that Riker was headed for the empty command area, the captain joined him. Together, they took their seats and settled in.

"Will," he said, his eyes trained on the forward viewscreen, "this time-shifting business . . . when it happens, I experience a moment of disorientation. If this should occur during a crisis, I want you to be ready to take command immediately."

There was no reaction. Turning to his first officer, Picard saw the faraway look on his face.

"Number One?"

Abruptly, Riker realized that the captain was looking at him. He straightened in his seat.

"Sorry, Captain. Be prepared to take command. Aye, sir."

But a moment later, it was clear that he was still absorbed by something—and Picard was willing to wager it had nothing to do with his duties.

The captain frowned. "Speaking of disorientation . . . are you all right, Will?"

The first officer nodded reassuringly. "Just a little distracted. I'm fine, sir. Really."

Picard didn't quite believe him, but he decided not to pursue the matter. Even Will Riker was allowed a daydream now and then. If an emergency arose, the captain had no fear that his exec would respond to it.

Besides, Picard told himself, I have to get some work done—before I pop out of this time period again. It sounded silly when he put it that way, but right now he had to juxtapose the unfathomable with the very mundane.

"You have the bridge, Number One. I'll be in my ready room."

Riker turned and smiled at him in a perfunctory way. "Aye, sir."

Rising, the captain made his way to his ready-room door. It slid aside at his approach, and the room itself was revealed to him.

As never before, he was grateful for the sanctumlike nature of it . . . the steady, predictable peacefulness. Everything was right where he expected it to be, from his antique Shakespearean folio to his model of the *Stargazer* . . . from his Naikous statue, acquired on the

Federation planet Kurlan, to his majestic Terran lionfish.

It was very heartening . . . and very much an illusion, in that regard. There was no guarantee that he'd be here an hour from now, or even a minute. Anyway, what significance could those terms have when one was weaving in and out of Time?

But enough of such mind-bending concerns. Right here, right now, Picard sat down behind his desk and applied himself to the ship's affairs. After all, life on the *Enterprise* had a way of going on, no matter what dangers might emerge in its path.

Yet he had barely begun when he heard the sound of chimes, notifying him that there was someone outside his door. Turning in that direction, he said, "Come."

As the door slid away, it showed him his chief medical officer. He thought he saw a look of concern on her face, but she was moving across the room too quickly for him to be sure.

Stopping by the replicator, she made her request. "Milk . . . warm. A dash of nutmeg."

The replicator hummed for a moment, then produced the required beverage. Taking it away, Beverly brought it to the captain.

He looked up at her. "What's this?"

She smiled. "A prescription. A glass of warm milk and eight hours' uninterrupted sleep."

Picard sat back in his chair. "Beverly . . ."

"Doctor's orders," she insisted. "You're exhausted. I don't know if you've slept in the past or the future, but I know you haven't slept in the present. Now, get some rest, or I'll have you relieved and sedated."

The captain chuckled, resigned to his fate. "Yes, *sir.*"

For a second or so, they just looked at each other, sharing the humor of the moment. Then Beverly leaned forward and put her hand on his.

It began as a friendly gesture, or so Picard thought. But the doctor left it there a beat longer than necessary, giving it a little squeeze before she lifted it again.

And as she straightened, he saw what he was now *certain* was a look of concern. The captain gazed into her eyes, trying to divine her thoughts.

"What's wrong?" he asked.

She seemed on the verge of telling him. Then, apparently thinking better of the idea, she turned and headed for the door. Picard stood, refusing to let the matter lie—whatever it was.

"Beverly!"

She stopped at the sound of her name, took a breath, and finally turned again to look at him. It took her a moment to gather herself before she could speak.

"As a physician," she said softly, "it's often my job to give people unpleasant news . . . to tell them that they need surgery or that they can't have children . . . or that they might be facing a very *difficult* illness . . ."

Before the doctor could finish, something seemed to catch in her throat. She looked away from him, her eyes bright. The captain moved to her, touched by her concern.

"You said yourself it's only a possibility," he reminded her. "Only one among many."

"But you've been to the future," she countered. "You *know* it's going to happen."

He smiled as best he could. "I prefer to think of the

future as something that is not written in stone. Beverly, a lot of things can happen in twenty-five years."

He wasn't sure how she would respond to that. The last thing he expected was that she would lean forward and kiss him on the lips. And yet, that is the very thing she did.

What's more, he kissed her back. And it was not like another kiss they had shared, several months earlier, after they had been linked mind-to-mind on the planet Kesprit. This time, it *lingered.*

And when it was over, Beverly looked into his eyes meaningfully. He could smell her perfume, subtle though it was. He had never realized how . . . provocative it could be.

"You're right," she said. "A lot of things can happen."

Before Picard could ask for an explanation, she turned and left—and this time he made no effort to stop her. As his ready-room door closed behind her, he contemplated what had just happened.

Was this the beginning of a new stage in their relationship? Or just a fleeting emotion, born of Beverly's concern for him?

Only Time would tell.

Remembering the glass of milk she'd brought him, he went back to his desk, picked it up, and took a sip. It was just as soothing, just as calming as the doctor had suggested.

Then, replacing the glass on his desk, he moved to the couch and stretched out. He could hear his joints creak with gratitude.

Beverly was right. He was exhausted. Closing his eyes, the captain assured himself that it would be only a short nap . . . in which he would no doubt revisit the kiss he had just shared, searching for its meaning. But then, there were less pleasant things to dream about, weren't there?

As he began to drift off, he thought he heard a voice. But that was ridiculous. He was alone in here. . . .

"Sir? Wake up, sir."

There was no denying the summons now. Opening his eyes, Picard looked for the source of it—and saw that La Forge was standing over him. There was some sort of light source behind him, making it difficult to get a good look at the man.

"Yes," he murmured. "Yes . . . what is it? Have we reached the Neutral Zone yet?"

La Forge scrutinized him with his artificial eyes. "The . . . Neutral Zone, Captain?"

That's when Picard sat up and looked around—and realized that he was back in Data's library. Back in the *future*.

And the light source behind La Forge was just a window through which they were receiving the late-afternoon light. Picard rubbed his eyes.

"Sorry," he said. "I was . . . in the past again." Sitting up, he gathered his senses. "What's going on?"

The younger man smiled sympathetically. "Data's arranged for us to run some tests on you in the biometrics lab. We're ready to go if you are."

Picard shook his head, remembering what he'd learned. "No . . . no, we don't have time for that. We have to get to the Neutral Zone."

La Forge's forehead wrinkled. "Why's that, sir?"

The older man tried to concentrate. "In the other two time periods, Starfleet reported a . . . um, some kind of . . . spatial anomaly in the . . . in the Devron system!" Exultant, he smacked his fist into the palm of his other hand. "That's it. The Devron system in the Neutral Zone."

La Forge sighed. "Sir . . ."

But Picard wouldn't let him go on. He was going strong now, and he didn't dare pause or he might lose his train of thought.

"If the anomaly was in the past . . . it might be here, too. We need to go find out if . . ."

The other man looked at him askance. "Just because you've seen it in two other time frames doesn't mean it's going to be here."

Picard felt the blood rush to his face. "Dammit, Geordi—I *know* what we have to do!"

La Forge smiled again. In a way, the older man thought, that was almost worse than the other look he'd given him. He could put up with doubts, with skepticism. But he couldn't stand being patronized.

"Okay, Captain. Whatever you say. But first of all, there *is* no Neutral Zone . . . remember?"

No Neutral Zone? Picard pondered the matter, plumbing his memory . . . and was surprised to realize that his friend was right.

"Klingons," he muttered. "In this time period, the Klingons have taken over the Romulan Empire. . . ."

La Forge nodded. "That's right. And relations between us and the Klingons aren't real cozy right now."

Getting irritated at his companion's tone, the older

man struggled to his feet. "I *know* that," he barked, pulling down on his tunic as he'd once pulled down on the front of his uniform. "I haven't *completely* lost my mind, you know."

Abruptly, it occurred to him how cantankerous he sounded. Again, he was running roughshod over those who were trying to help him. Hoping to take the edge off his remark, he put his hand on La Forge's shoulder.

"Sorry, Geordi. When I'm here, it's hard for me to concentrate . . . and remember things. I don't mean to take out that frustration on you."

The younger man nodded. "It's okay." A beat. "Well, if we're going to the Devron system, we're going to need a ship."

Picard scratched his chin. "We will, at that." Then it struck him how they might get one. "I think it's time to call in some old favors."

La Forge raised an eyebrow. "Favors?" he repeated.

"Yes," confirmed Picard. "Contact Admiral Riker at Starbase Two-Four-Seven."

Geordi gazed approvingly at the monitor that Data had brought into the library. Except for the Starfleet insignia, the image on the screen was an unbroken field of violet-blue.

"Nice resolution," he said appraisingly. "To tell you the truth, I've never seen one like this in a private home."

Data nodded. "As I indicated earlier, holding the Lucasian Chair does have its perquisites."

It appeared there was a whole *slew* of perquisites, because it hadn't taken the android long to contact Starfleet Command—or, having contacted them, to arrange for an audience with Admiral Riker.

A moment later, only minutes after Data had made his request, Riker got in touch with them. The man was a lot grayer than Geordi remembered—but then, who among his old comrades wasn't? And as an admiral, the man had a whole lot more responsibility than before—a whole lot more reasons for his hair to have gone gray.

But that wasn't the only difference in him. Even before Riker opened his mouth to speak, he seemed brittle, somehow . . . less easygoing than the man Geordi had known on the *Enterprise.* And there was no trace at all of that trademark Will Riker smile.

"Jean-Luc," said the admiral, acknowledging his former captain. "Data . . . Geordi." He was clearly pleased to see them, but he didn't show all the enthusiasm that Picard had probably been hoping for. Riker almost seemed . . . well, *leery* of what this might be about.

"Will," replied Picard. "You look every inch the admiral. I knew we'd move you up in the ranks eventually."

Riker shifted uncomfortably in his seat. "Of course you did," he agreed, but in a way that said he didn't have time for this. "Now, what can I do for you, sir?"

As Picard outlined his needs and the reasons for them, the admiral's demeanor became frostier by degrees. Finally, he sat back in his chair and frowned.

"Jean-Luc," he said, "you know I'd like to help . . .

but frankly, what you're asking for is impossible. The Klingons have closed their borders to all Federation starships."

Obviously trying to remain patient, the captain shook his head. "I don't think you appreciate the . . . the gravity of the situation. Will, if this . . . this spatial anomaly really *is* in the Devron system . . ."

Riker didn't let him finish. "I saw a report from Starfleet Intelligence on that sector this morning. There's no unusual activity in the Devron system . . . nothing out of the ordinary in terms of celestial phenomena."

"I don't believe that!" snapped the older man. "Maybe their long-range scanners are flawed. We have to go there, see for ourselves!"

The admiral looked reluctant to turn Picard down flat. He eyed Data. "Professor, what do *you* make of all this?"

The android seemed to hesitate for a moment, considering his answer carefully. Data had come a long way, it seemed to Geordi. He no longer made decisions based purely on logic; now, he appeared to take people's feelings into account.

"I am not certain," the android said at last. "However, I cannot disprove what the captain is saying. And he seems to be *convinced* he is traveling back and forth through time."

Riker frowned. "Right." Clearly, Data was siding with Picard—and that made it harder for him to dismiss the matter. "Look," he said, "I've got the *Yorktown* out near the border. I'll have Captain Shelby run some long-range scans of the Devron system. If she finds anything, I'll let you know."

The captain shook his head. "No. That's not good enough."

"It'll have to be," responded the admiral. "I'm sorry, Jean-Luc. That's all I can do. Riker out."

CHAPTER 11

As his monitor went dark, Riker sat back in his chair and sighed. He hated to be so brusque with a man who had done for him what Jean-Luc Picard had done.

Still, what choice did he have? The captain might as well have asked for a pet mugato as request permission to enter Klingon territory. Neither one was likely to ensure him a long life.

Though, judging by the looks of him, Picard wasn't going to enjoy a very long life anyway. And what was left to him was going to be full of misery and humiliation, thanks to his disease.

Was that it? the admiral wondered. Was this the captain's way of going out in a blaze of glory—instead of slowly and painfully deteriorating over time?

Riker thought about it—and ultimately rejected the idea. It would be one thing for Picard to sacrifice his own life. But Data and Geordi had been willing to go with him, and the captain would never have sacrificed their lives as well.

Speaking of Data . . . what was it with his hair? It looked like he'd used his head to erase one of those blackboards still in use at Cambridge.

The monitor beeped. "Riker here," he responded mechanically.

An instant later, he saw the clean-cut visage of Captain Sam Lavelle. The man smiled, genuinely glad to see the officer who had been so hard on him when he'd joined the *Enterprise*.

"Admiral Riker. You're looking well, sir. But then, we Canadians are an enduring breed."

It was a joke, of course. Lavelle had once made the mistake of thinking Riker was from Canada. Actually, he was born and bred in Alaska.

"So we are," said the admiral, acknowledging the attempt at humor. Unfortunately, he didn't much feel like laughing right now.

Lavelle's demeanor became more serious as he noticed his superior's lack of enthusiasm. "Something wrong, sir?"

Riker shrugged. "Make me a promise, Sam. If I come to you when I'm ninety years old and ask you to ferry me somewhere in the *Enterprise* . . . somewhere crazy, where I'm likely to get myself and the rest of the crew killed . . . let me down easy, all right?"

Lavelle looked at him, obviously unable to divine the reason for the request. However, he must have sensed it wasn't really a topic the admiral wanted to discuss.

"First off," he replied, "I don't think you'd ask for

something like that . . . not at any age. And second, it'll
be someone else's problem—or have you forgotten what
day this is?"

Abruptly, Riker remembered. "That's right. You're
retiring today, aren't you?"

"You sound so glum," the younger man observed,
deriving pleasure from the fact. "Does that mean you're
having second thoughts?"

Another old joke. The admiral reacted as Lavelle
would have expected.

"No, Sam. I still think you make lousy officer material.
It's just that I've gotten used to you. You know what they
say about old dogs and new tricks."

Lavelle smiled. "Then you're not sorry you listened
to—" He stopped himself, realizing he'd made a mistake by starting down that path. "Sorry," he said. "I
didn't mean to bring her up."

Riker nodded, trying to ignore the pain of remem-
brance. "It's all right," he lied. Then, changing the
subject: "So you really think you're going to be happy
running a research colony?"

Now it was Sam's turn to shrug. "I promised Korina
that we'd try something different for a while—and this
is what she chose. After keeping her penned up on the
Enterprise for fifteen years, I don't really get much of a
say in the matter." He smiled. "And then again, maybe
I've had enough of the shipboard life myself. I guess I'm
more of a landlubber than I ever cared to admit."

Riker eyed him affectionately. "I'm going to miss you,
Lavelle. You're sure I can't talk you out of this?"

The younger man shook his head. "Too late. My bags

are already packed." He gazed at the admiral. "And what about you? How long are you going to stay in that dusty old office of yours?"

"Until they kick me out of it," the older man quipped.

"And not before?" Sam pressed, a little mischievously. "Are you saying you don't get the urge anymore to hop on a starship and see faraway places? To go where no one has gone before?"

It was a good question, even if it was posed half in jest. Riker took a breath, let it out.

"Faraway places," he said, surprising himself with the note of bitterness in his voice, "don't mean quite as much as they used to, somehow. Maybe I'm getting old."

For what might have been the first time since their conversation began, Lavelle spoke in earnest. "Maybe you're *letting* yourself get old," he suggested.

Yet another subject the admiral wasn't eager to delve into. "Tell your people I'll have a replacement in a day or two, Sam. And keep in touch, dammit. From what I hear, Beta Retimnion is as accessible by subspace as anywhere else in the galaxy."

The younger man smiled, though a bit wistfully. "That works both ways, sir. I'll see you around. And thanks again . . . for everything. Lavelle out."

Again, the screen went dark, and Riker leaned back into his seat. It was a sobering moment when a man ten years his junior had the temerity to retire from the center seat.

Where had the years gone? And how had he gotten so far away from the thing he loved best . . . the search for adventure that had propelled him into space in the first place?

He wished he could turn back the clock a quarter-century, when things were different . . . when he had everything he wanted and nothing to feel guilty about. What he wouldn't do to have those days back again. . . .

As the communication with Admiral Riker came to an end, Geordi sighed. This wasn't going to sit well with the captain. But on the other hand, it was clearly for the best.

After all, they had no business trying to make their way through Klingon territory. They weren't the confident young officers they used to be—and even if they had been, they would have been risking a lot to satisfy an old man's fantasy.

As he watched, Picard turned his back on the monitor. It wasn't difficult to divine his emotions. He was frustrated and he was angry—and worse than that, he felt betrayed by a man he'd once thought of as a son.

But he would get over it. Geordi would take him home and see to that. A couple of days from now, he would forget he had ever attached any importance at all to the Devron system.

"Damn him, anyway," growled Picard. "Ungrateful young pup. He's been sitting behind that desk too long. Do you know how many times I pulled his chestnuts out of the fire? Do you?"

"Well," said Geordi, trying hard to mask his relief, "I guess all we can do now is wait . . . and see if the *Yorktown* finds anything."

Data turned to him and replied, "There is another option."

Geordi sighed. Another option was the *last* thing he wanted right now.

"And that is?" he inquired.

"We could arrange passage aboard a medical ship," explained the android.

"A medical ship?" echoed Picard, his eyes narrowing.

Data nodded. "There was an outbreak of Terellian plague on Romulus. The Klingon High Council has been allowing Federation medical ships to cross the border."

The captain grinned. "Yes . . . yes, of course . . ."

Geordi eyed Data. It looked like this was going to go on, after all.

"So I guess all we need now is a medical ship," he said.

The older man grabbed the android by the arm. "I think I can arrange that, Mr. Data. Find the *U.S.S. Pasteur.* I have some . . . some *pull* with her commanding officer."

For a moment, he seemed lost in thought, his eyes glazed over with memories. Then he came out of it.

"At least," he amended, "I used to. . . ."

The former Beverly Crusher, captain of the medical vessel known as the *U.S.S. Pasteur,* considered all three of the visitors standing there in her ready room. However, she focused most of her attention on the man she had once called her husband.

"I never could say no to you," she told Jean-Luc, leaning back in her chair.

He smiled. "You should have said it when I asked you to marry me."

Beverly looked at him with mock annoyance. "Don't

bring that up," she said, "or I'll change my mind about all this."

For a moment, a scene flashed before her eyes. She saw herself on her wedding day, before the Howard family house on Caldos. She and Jean-Luc were standing before Governor Maturin, taking their vows as their friends and fellow officers looked on . . . and the wind brought the scent of heather.

Wesley was there, showing no outward signs of the strange and wonderful being he had become. He was smiling, happy for her.

Jean-Luc's brother, Robert, was happy as well—glad to see that their marriage would start off in a place blessed with tradition. Or so he had told them, in a private moment before the ceremony.

No doubt, he would have liked it better if the ground had been French, and the house that of his own family . . . and the scent on the wind that of sun-ripened grapes. But then, he'd been expecting something cold and artificial—so an homage to *any* tradition was a pleasant surprise.

And Beverly herself was happy—truly happy, for the first time in many years. She felt as if, with her marriage to this fine and noble man, some cosmic balance had been restored. And this time, she vowed on that special day, it would last.

So much for her powers of prognostication, she thought sourly, as her thoughts returned to the bridge of the *Pasteur*. It was a good thing she was a doctor, and not a fortune-teller.

Jean-Luc elbowed Data in his synthetic ribs. "You see?" he said. "I knew I could still count on her . . . not like Riker." His expression turned bitter as he recalled his discussion with the admiral. "Did I tell you what he said to me, Beverly? To *me?*"

She nodded. "You told me, Jean-Luc."

It hurt her to see him like this—a man whose intellect was once so engaging—reduced now to near-senility. She took in Geordi and then Data with a glance.

"Well, then. The first order of business is to obtain clearance to cross the Klingon border. And believe me, that won't be easy."

"What about *Worf?*" asked the former chief engineer. "Isn't he still on the Klingon High Council?"

"I'm not sure," responded Data. "Information on the Klingon political structure is hard to come by these days. However, at last report, Worf was living on H'atoria—a small Klingon colony near the border."

Jean-Luc snapped his fingers. "Worf . . . yes, that's it . . . that's the answer." He nodded. *"Worf.* He'll help us. Let's make it so."

Abruptly, her conn officer's voice cut in over the intercom. "Chilton to Captain Picard."

"Picard here," replied Beverly.

"Go ahead," said the man she'd been married to, responding to the same summons.

They exchanged looks.

"Captain," said Chilton, apparently unperturbed by the confused answer from the ready room, "McKinley Station is signaling. They want to know when we'll be docking."

Beverly stood. "Tell McKinley that we've been called away on a priority mission. We won't be docking any time soon."

"Aye, sir," came Chilton's acknowledgment.

As the captain of the *Pasteur* headed for the door, her former mate smiled at her. "Kept the name?" he asked.

Ignoring the question, which wasn't really a question at all, Beverly led Jean-Luc and his companions out onto the bridge. If she needed any reminders of what the *Pasteur*'s purpose was, she found it in the caduceus motif liberally displayed around her center seat.

For now, she reflected, the ship would have a slightly different purpose. But then, if Jean-Luc's judgment could be trusted, they would still be saving lives.

"Nell," she said, addressing Ensign Chilton, "lay in a course for H'atoria. Best speed."

Chilton glanced back over her shoulder, but didn't display any surprise at the order. "Aye, Captain."

Turning to Jean-Luc, Beverly gestured to the turbolift. "I've prepared quarters for you on deck five if you'd like some rest."

He shot a sour look at her. "There you go again, always telling me to get some rest. I wanted a wife, not a personal physician."

Smiling cordially, she reminded him of where he was—and who was in charge here. "I could have you escorted there," she told him.

For a moment, she thought he would make this harder than it had to be. Then, making a sound of disgust, Jean-Luc turned his back on her. "I can find my way around a starship, Beverly. I'm not *that* old. . . ."

And, grumbling all the way, he entered the turbolift.

"Everyone treats me like an invalid," he muttered,

looking about the lift compartment, as if there were someone there to listen to him. "But I've still got a few years left . . . don't need to be led around . . . shown everything . . ."

A moment later, the doors closed behind him. As soon as he was out of sight, Beverly turned to Geordi and Data. She was hard-pressed to keep the sadness out of her voice.

"How long since he's had a neurological scan?" she inquired.

Geordi shrugged; his artificial eyes glittered back at her. "I'm not sure, but don't waste your time suggesting it. He says he's not taking 'any more damn tests.'"

Beverly grunted. That sounded just like him. "Do you believe he's doing what he says he's doing? That he's moving through time?"

At that, Geordi looked away. It was clear he didn't put much faith in Jean-Luc's story.

"I don't know if I do, either," she confided. "But he's still Jean-Luc Picard. And if he wants to go on one more mission, that's what we're damned well going to do."

Inside the turbolift, Picard grumbled to himself, fixing his objective in his mind. "Got to find that anomaly . . . show them all I'm not crazy. They'll see. . . ."

They would, too. And then they would be embarrassed at having doubted him.

Not that he cared all that much about being proven right. That would just be the icing on the cake. What he really wanted was to find out why he was shifting through time . . . and what it had to do with the phenomenon in the Devron system.

Abruptly, the lift stopped and the doors opened. He stepped out . . .

. . . onto the bridge. For a moment, Picard had that feeling of dizziness again—of disorientation. Then he realized what had happened. Once again, he'd been transported in time somehow.

Looking around, he saw Tasha at tactical . . . Worf at an aft station . . . O'Brien at conn and Data at ops. Troi was sitting in her customary seat beside the captain's chair.

Pulling down on the front of his tunic, Picard intoned, "Report."

"We're on course for Farpoint," Troi replied. "We should arrive in approximately fourteen hours, thirty minutes."

He nodded. Moving to O'Brien's side, he gazed over the man's shoulder at the helm console monitors.

The chief looked up at him uncomfortably. "Is there something I can do for you, sir?"

"There is," the captain confirmed crisply. "How far are we from the Chavez system?"

O'Brien peered at him through narrowed eyes. "The Chavez system? We just passed it, sir."

Picard found himself staring. "Passed it . . . and nothing happened?"

The chief looked quizzical. "Nothing, sir."

The captain cursed inwardly. "Drop out of warp," he ordered. "Reverse course. Take us back to the Chavez system."

He could see the reactions to his directive out of the corner of his eye. Tasha, Troi, and several others were having a hard time figuring him out. O'Brien, however, simply did as he was told.

It took several minutes for them to come about and return to the coordinates Picard had in mind. Of course, considering the circumstances, it seemed like much longer.

Finally, the chief spoke up again. "We've entered the Chavez system, sir."

The captain turned to Data. "Commander . . . is there anything unusual in the vicinity?"

The android looked back at him. "How would you define *unusual,* sir? Every region of space has unique properties that cannot be found anywhere else."

Picard thought about it—trying to piece it together the way it happened the *first* time. Finally, he came up with something.

"There should be a barrier of some sort," he recalled. "A large plasma field . . . highly disruptive."

Tasha worked at her tactical board. After a while, she shook her head. "Nothing, sir."

Frustrated, the captain looked down again at O'Brien's console. "It's the right time . . . the right place. He should *be* here."

O'Brien's brow puckered. "Who, sir?"

Straightening, Picard looked around the bridge—and called out. *"Q!* We're here, dammit!"

There was no answer.

Again, he addressed his nemesis. "This has gone on long enough! What sort of game are you playing?"

Still no response—at least, not from Q.

The bridge crew was responding, however. They were exchanging glances from one to the other—no doubt starting to wonder about their captain's sanity.

Frowning, he turned to Troi. "Counselor, do you sense an alien presence of the sort I described earlier? A superior intelligence?"

She looked worried. "No, sir."

In the aft section, though they didn't think Picard noticed, Worf and Tasha were whispering back and forth.

"What is a . . . Q?" he asked.

She shrugged. "As far as I know, it's a letter of the alphabet."

Blast it, thought the captain, where *was* he? Where was his alien tormentor?

"This is not the way it's supposed to happen . . ." he muttered. Then he spoke in a louder, more authoritative voice. "Maintain position here," he told them. "I'll be in my ready room."

En route, he endured his officers' stares without a word. What could he say, after all? That the super-intelligent being he'd been expecting hadn't shown up? That he'd diverged from Starfleet orders to lead them on some kind of wild-goose chase?

Disgusted, he entered his ready room . . .

* * *

. . . and found himself in a different place entirely.

It was a courtroom of sorts, made of glass and steel, without a single surface that wasn't hard and unyielding. A crowd was packed into the place—a gallery of leering, hollow-eyed scarecrows, men and women who pointed at him and shrieked his name.

Among them were the same haggard souls he had seen in the vineyards of his "future" and in the shuttlebay of his "past"—except that their numbers had vastly multiplied. The air was rank with their scent, with their hatred and desperation.

Suddenly, he knew where he was—and when. He had been here before, after all. The time was the twenty-first century, the era of mankind's post-atomic horror.

That explained the hunger and the poverty that characterized the spectators . . . the bitterness in their voices, the hopelessness in their eyes.

And this venue was the one in which he had been placed on trial several years earlier. Not just him alone, either, but all of humanity.

As if to confirm his suspicions, everyone looked in one direction at once—at an entrance to the room, approachable only through a long, dark hallway. There was someone making his way down that hallway now— someone sitting cross-legged on a floating chair.

Q, thought the captain. Who else?

A moment later he was proven right. With impeccable timing, the entity emerged from the shadows, playing the crowd like a virtuoso. The haggard ones roared their approval as Q wafted out to the center of the room, wearing an elaborate set of judge's robes.

Holding his hand up, he quieted the cheering throng. Finally, there was silence—utter and complete. With a supercilious smile on his face, Q turned to Picard.

"Mon capitaine," he said, his eyes twinkling with irony. "I thought you'd *never* get here."

CHAPTER **12**

"Q," said the captain. "I thought so."

The entity shrugged. "Actually, you were only about ninety-six percent certain of it . . . but why quibble?"

Picard had no patience for Q's antics. "What's going on?" he demanded.

"Isn't it obvious, Jean-Luc?" Q made an expansive gesture, indicating the entire courtroom and its cadre of foul-smelling occupants. "Can't you see for yourself, old bean? Or is a little simple cognition beyond you?"

The captain frowned. He would have to play the game, apparently, like it or not. "The last time I stood in this courtroom was seven years ago. . . ."

"Seven years ago," Q repeated mockingly. "How little you mortals understand time. Must you be so linear, Jean-Luc?"

Doggedly, Picard went on. "You accused me of being the representative of a barbarous species. . . ."

"I believe the exact words were 'a dangerous, savage child-race,' were they not?"

"But we demonstrated that mankind has become peaceful and benevolent," the captain insisted. "You agreed, and let us go on our way." He looked around at the crowd of silent, glaring onlookers. "Why do I find myself back in this courtroom now, when our business here is finished?"

Q sighed. "You need me to connect the dots for you, I see. Lead you from A to B, B to C, and so on . . . so your puny mind can comprehend." He shook his head wearily, vexed by man's limitations. "How boring . . ."

"For you, perhaps. But—"

"It would be so much more entertaining," Q mused, "if you tried to figure this out." He snapped his fingers, his eyes widening as if seized all of a sudden by an idea. "In fact," he said, "I'll help you out."

Reaching under his robes, he pulled out a small flipboard containing white cards. The first one had a large numeral 10 on it.

"Here's the deal, *mon ami*. I'll answer any question that calls for a yes or a no. Put it together in ten questions or less . . . and you, Jean-Luc Picard, could be our big winner. What do you say?"

The captain didn't seem to have much of a choice. "All right, Q." He tried to establish as much as possible right from the beginning. "Are you putting mankind on trial again?"

Q smiled. "No," he said genially, flipping a card over to reveal the numeral 9.

"Is there any connection at all," inquired Picard,

"between the trial seven years ago and whatever's going on now?"

Q pretended to think about that one. "Now, let's see. Hmmmmm . . . I would have to say . . . *yes.*" He flipped to the card that showed 8.

"Yet you say we're not on trial again. . . ."

"That's correct," said Q. "The trial is long over. That's three questions for the contestant from Earth."

The captain protested. "That was a statement, not a question!"

Unmoved, Q flipped another card over. "Seven to go. And not a very good job so far, if I may say so. A chimp could probably have done better—and been more witty in the process."

Frustrated, Picard concentrated on his next question. "The spatial anomaly in the Neutral Zone . . . is it related to what's happening?"

"Oh," said Q, "most definitely *yes.*" He flipped yet another card.

"Is it part of a Romulan plot? A ploy to start a war?"

"You've been spending too much time with the Klingon," Q observed. "No . . . and no again. Six down and only four to go."

"Wait a minute," argued the captain. "That's only five."

Q ticked off the questions on his fingers. " 'Is it a Romulan plot? Is it a ploy to start a war?' Those are separate questions."

Picard held his anger in check. This was an opportunity to get to the bottom of this. He dared not waste it.

"Did you create the anomaly, Q?"

The entity laughed merrily. "No, no, no, my incredible dullard of a starship captain. You're going to be so surprised when you realize where it came from. That is, if you ever manage to figure it out. And you have only three questions left."

The captain decided to try another tack. "Are you responsible for my shifting through time?"

Q looked around, as if he was about to do something illegal and was concerned that someone might be watching. He leaned down from his perch atop the floating cushion.

"I'll answer that if you promise you won't tell anyone," he breathed.

"I promise," the human told him.

"In that case," Q whispered, *"yes."*

Picard shook his head. "But why?"

"I'm sorry," said Q. "That's not a yes-or-no question. You forfeit the rest of the game." Giddily, he tossed away the flipboard. "I expected as much, you know. And, as I might point out, that's a perfect example of why we've made our decision."

The captain shot him a questioning look. "Your decision?" he echoed.

Q nodded. "The verdict has been decided, Captain. You're guilty."

Picard took a half-step toward his adversary. "Guilty of what?"

"Of being inferior, of course." Q looked at him with unconcealed contempt. "Seven years ago, I said we'd be watching you. And we have been. We've been watching and hoping that your apelike race would demonstrate some modicum of growth . . . give us some indication that your minds have the capacity for further expansion."

Q's floating cushion lowered so that his eyes were on a level with the captain's. There was a hard-edged disdain in them that Picard had never seen there before.

"And what have we seen instead?" the entity went on. "You spent your time worrying about Commander Riker's career . . . listening to Counselor Troi's pedantic psychobabble . . . helping Worf determine if he's a man or a mouse . . . and indulging Data in his witless exploration of humanity."

"We have journeyed to countless new worlds," Picard maintained. "We have made contact with new species . . . expanded the Federation's understanding of the universe . . ."

"In your own paltry, limited way," Q conceded. "But you have no idea how far you still have to go. And instead of using the past seven years to change and grow—you have squandered them."

"I beg to differ . . ." he began.

Q dismissed his comment with a wave of his hand. "Time in the universe may be eternal, Captain. However, the patience of our Continuum is not—and you and your kind have exhausted it."

It sounded to Picard as if this was a battle he couldn't hope to win. It seemed that Q had already made his decision.

"And having rendered a verdict," he asked, "have you decided upon a sentence?"

"Indeed," replied Q. "You see, it's time to end your

trek through the stars, Jean-Luc. It's time for you to make room for other, more worthy species."

The captain didn't quite understand. "You mean we're to be denied travel through space?"

Q's eyes flashed fire. "No, you obtuse piece of flotsam. You're to be denied *existence*. Humanity's fate has been sealed. You will be completely and irrevocably *destroyed*."

No, thought Picard. How could that be? Even a spiteful entity like Q was not capable of such an act.

"I?" responded Q, having intruded in the human's mind. "There you go again, blaming *me* for everything. Well, this time I'm not your enemy—even though I could easily have become one, after listening to that insipid balalaika music all evening."

"Balalaika music? I don't—"

"Never mind." He leaned in close to the captain, so close their noses were almost touching. "I'm not the one who causes the annihilation of mankind," said Q. *"You* are."

Picard shook his head. "Me . . . ?"

"That's right. You're doing it right now . . . you've already done it . . . and you will do it yet again in the future."

The captain felt his teeth grate together. "What sort of meaningless double-talk is that?"

Q took a long, melodramatic draft of air and slowly let it out. "Oh, my. He doesn't understand. I have only myself to blame, I suppose. I believed in him . . . thought he had some tiny spark of potential. But apparently, I was wrong about him. *C'est la vie.*"

"No," said Picard, sensing that the entity was about to make his exit. "You can't just leave it at that. You've got to—"

Q didn't even seem to hear him. "Good luck, Jean-Luc. Maybe you can still avoid killing every humanoid in the galaxy . . . but I doubt it."

"No!" cried the captain.

"May whatever god you believe in have mercy on your soul. This court stands adjourned."

Again, louder this time: "No!"

But Q was already raising his hand, signaling an end to his audience. There was the crash of a gong . . .

. . . and Picard sat up, fully awake. It wasn't until the sound had faded away to nothing that he realized he was in his ready room. And it took a moment longer than that for him to remember that he was in the "present."

Bolting to his feet, he made his way to the door and emerged onto the bridge. Seeing that Riker wasn't there, he looked up to the intercom grid.

"Commander Riker," he said.

"Riker here," came the reply.

"Assemble the senior staff," the captain told him, shivering at what he had just learned. "And go to red alert. We have a bigger problem on our hands than we thought."

CHAPTER 13

"Dr. Pulaski?"

Kate Pulaski looked up from her solitary table, where she'd been playing the Andorian game of *choctoq*—and losing. She wasn't sure whom she expected to see . . . but it wasn't the Daughter of the Fifth House of Betazed, Holder of the Sacred Chalice of Riix.

"Ambassador Troi?" she responded, unable to keep the surprise out of her voice. A few of her fellow officers looked up from the surrounding tables and then went back to their own conversations.

Lwaxana Troi hadn't changed much in the five years since the doctor had seen her last. Her hair was a dusky red instead of brunette, but she still had that friskiness about her that sent strong captains sprinting wildly for the escape pods.

Then again, Pulaski thought, who am *I* to talk about other people being frisky? Those who've been to the trough as often as I have shouldn't throw stones . . . to mix a metaphor.

"I see you remember me," commented the Betazoid. "And yes, I *have* changed the color of my hair. How sweet of you to notice."

Pulaski reddened. Telepathy was a damned inconvenient trait, when you came right down to it. Gesturing to the chair on the other side of the table, she said, "Please, sit down."

The ambassador sat. Picking up one of the *choctoq* tiles, she inspected the dragonlike symbol on its smooth, white face. "I know," she began. "You're wondering what I'm doing here on the *Repulse.* Well, Ambassador Zul of Triannis took ill just a few days ago . . ."

"And you took his place on the Alpha Tiberia negotiating team," the chief medical officer finished. "I've got it. But Ambassador Zul was one of our foremost experts on Ferengi barter techniques. . . ."

"So he was," Lwaxana agreed, replacing the tile in its starburst configuration. "Which is why they asked *me* to take his place. You see, I've had some dealings of my own with the Ferengi. And let me assure you, Doctor, they were a lot more colorful than Ambassador Zul's."

Pulaski smiled. "I have no doubt of it. So, tell me . . . how's Deanna? And the rest of the *Enterprise* crew?"

The Betazoid frowned. "You may not believe it, but Deanna's still not married. And she's got the prettiest face on that entire ship, if I say so myself." She sighed. "As for the others . . . they're about the same, I suppose." She thought for a moment. "Did Will Riker have a beard when you were with them?"

Seven years in his past, Captain Jean-Luc Picard (Patrick Stewart) struggles to understand the reason for his strange journey through time.

In a vineyard in the south of France, 25 years in his future, Captain Picard begins to realize he has traveled through time.

Captain Picard explains his odd journey to Geordi La Forge (LeVar Burton), his former chief engineer.

In his study in England, Professor Data (Brent Spiner)
considers Captain Picard's request for aid.

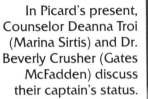

In Picard's present, Counselor Deanna Troi (Marina Sirtis) and Dr. Beverly Crusher (Gates McFadden) discuss their captain's status.

An older Worf (Michael Dorn), now governing a Klingon colony, considers his former captain's request to join him on one last mission.

Seven years in Captain Picard's past, Miles O'Brien (Colm Meaney) wonders at the strange actions of his new commander.

A troubled Captain Beverly Picard commands the medical ship *U.S.S. Pasteur.*

Lieutenant Commander Data and Chief Engineer La Forge apply their technical expertise to the problem threatening mankind.

Captain Picard begs his ex-wife, Beverly, for help in his mission.

Worf and Lieutenant Tasha Yar (Denise Crosby) are perplexed by the strange behavior of their new captain.

Captain Picard faces down Q (John DeLancie) as the fate of
the universe hangs in the balance.

The doctor nodded. "He'd just grown it."

"And . . . did you meet Alexander?"

Pulaski shook her head. "The name doesn't ring a bell. Who's he?"

Lwaxana smiled. "Just the most precious little Klingon child you ever saw. It's hard to believe his father is someone as grim as Mr. Woof."

The doctor looked at her, amused. "You mean *Worf.*"

"Woof, Worf . . ." She shrugged, as if the difference were insignificant. "In any case, Alexander came aboard after his poor mother died. Did you know K'Ehleyr?"

Pulaski put *cha'* and *cha'* together. "K'Ehleyr was the boy's mother?"

The Betazoid nodded. "Poor dear. She was killed by some horrid High Council member, when her research threatened to expose his family's treachery."

The doctor shivered. "How awful. But the boy is all right?"

"He is *now,"* Lwaxana told her. "Thanks to the attention my daughter showers on him."

Pulaski had liked Worf—but she couldn't picture him raising a youngster all on his own. It had to be hard on someone like him.

"It is," the ambassador replied.

Again, Pulaski had reason to regret the development of telepathy in Betazoids. "And Data?" she asked. "How's *he* doing?"

Lwaxana looked at her. "The android?" She considered the question. "Actually, he doesn't seem to change much, does—" She stopped herself. "No, I take that back. He doesn't change *physically*. But now that I think about it, his personality has developed quite a bit. He's become more socially adept. More . . . human, I'd say, for lack of a better word."

The doctor sighed and looked down at the primary-colored *choctoq* pieces on her side of the table. "I was so wrong."

"About what?" asked the ambassador.

"About Data," she answered. "When I was on the *Enterprise,* I really believed he was just a fancy bucket of bolts. After all, he wasn't a biological entity, and I didn't think there was any other kind. But I've been accessing his Starfleet personnel file from time to time, and I see now that I was off the mark." She grunted philosophically. "Way off."

Lwaxana regarded her. "You ought to tell him so. I bet he'd like to hear it from someone like you. Someone he respects."

Pulaski nodded. "Maybe I will. I don't know about him, but it'd sure as Shadrak make *me* feel better." She paused. "In fact, maybe I'll pay a little visit to the *Enterprise.* I've got some time coming, and—"

The Betazoid leaned forward and shook her head. "Not right now, dear," she said in a hushed tone.

Lwaxana looked around to make sure no one else in the rec room was looking. Then, satisfied that they had some privacy, she went on.

"The *Enterprise* is on a secret mission," she explained. "At the Romulan Neutral Zone. There's some sort of anomaly there—whatever that is."

The doctor eyed her. "But if it's secret, how do you . . . ?" And then she answered her own question. *Telepathy.*

The ambassador smiled. "It pays to hang around with an admiral now and then. You never know *what* you might find out." Suddenly, the smile disappeared. "Of course, I wouldn't want any of this to become common knowledge. Deanna would *kill* me—and Riix knows, the poor girl has enough problems. Did I tell you she's still unmarried?"

Pulaski grinned. "Yes, ma'am. I believe you did."

Lieutenant Reginald Barclay heaved a long, tremulous sigh as he remembered the details of his recent transformation.

"Actually," he said, "it wasn't so bad being a spider. I mean, I wasn't really aware of what was going on. I just had this general . . . I don't know, perception, I guess you'd call it . . . that things had changed. That they'd slowed down, somehow. Or that my reactions had speeded up. And . . . oh, yes. Then there was that *other* thing."

He turned to look at Counselor Troi. As ever, she was gazing at him sympathetically from her chair on the other side of the room.

"You mean the appetite for flies?" she suggested nonjudgmentally.

He nodded. Even now, it was hard for him to think of one without salivating just a little. "Yes. *That.*"

The counselor smiled. "As I've told you before, Reg, what you're feeling isn't at all abnormal. Everyone on the ship was affected by that protomorphosis disease. And everyone—myself included—has some unsettling memories of what happened to them while they were devolving."

He grunted. "Yes, but not everyone on the ship had the disease *named* after him."

Troi looked at him. "Dr. Crusher did that as a matter of scientific tradition. If you want her to change it . . ."

He pondered the possibility for a moment, then shook his head. Now that he thought about it, he sort of liked the idea, even if it did imply that he was to blame for the whole epidemic.

After all, it guaranteed him a certain immortality. For hundreds, maybe thousands of years, Federation doctors and scientists would be speaking of Barclay's proto-morphosis syndrome in reverential tones.

That is, if the Federation was still around. The way things were going, he wasn't so sure that would be the case.

"I guess the spider thing isn't what's *really* bothering me," he confessed. "Or even the fact that I've had a disease named after me."

The counselor had known that all along, of course, though she hadn't said so. That's how she worked, he mused.

Now, for instance, she was waiting patiently for him to tell her what the *real* problem was. Finally, he spoke up.

"It's this mission," he explained. "The anomaly that's been discovered in the Devron system . . . all those Warbirds that the Romulans have sent to the Neutral Zone." He tried to swallow back the trepidation he felt rising in his throat. "We had to fill out a combat-readiness report in engineering. You know what that means, don't you?"

Troi just returned his gaze. "No, Reg. What *does* it mean?"

He said it as calmly as he could. "That we're going to war with them. The Romulans, I mean." He looked down at his hands, which were shivering ever so slightly. "No one's come out and made an announcement, but I can see the handwriting on the wall."

The counselor leaned forward and took her time responding. For once, his anxiety had some solid basis in reality, and they both knew it.

"I think you're jumping to conclusions, Reg. I can't tell you for certain that there *won't* be a war. However, that's only one possible result."

Barclay frowned. "What about the combat-readiness reports? You don't ask for those unless you expect something to happen."

"Or expect that something *might* happen," she corrected. "As of right now, we don't know very much about the situation. We haven't figured out where the anomaly came from or why the Romulans have such an interest in it. So we're being cautious . . . until we *do* know."

That made him feel a little better—but not much. "But what if the Romulans react to *our* reaction? What if they see us coming and decide we've . . . um, misinterpreted what they've done?"

Troi's expression remained a tolerant one. "There's always that risk," she conceded. "But I wouldn't characterize the Romulans as an impulsive people . . . would you? It seems to me they'd think twice before initiating any hostile actions."

Barclay looked at her. "They sent thirty Warbirds to

the Neutral Zone. If they're not planning a hostile action, then why . . . ?" His fear rising to choke him, he found he couldn't finish the sentence.

"Reg," replied the counselor, "I don't know how this will turn out. I'm just saying that, until we have more information, there's no point in getting worried about it." She smiled reassuringly. "Besides, you know that Captain Picard will do everything in his power to avoid an armed conflict."

That much was true. But it seemed to the engineer that Picard might not have all that much control over the situation. Hell, he might not have *any* control at all.

He was about to point that out—but a voice on the intercom system filled the room before he had the chance.

"Riker to Counselor Troi. The captain's asked me to convene the senior staff in the observation lounge . . . *immediately.*"

The counselor seldom looked perturbed, Barclay told himself. But she looked perturbed *now.*

"On my way," she assured her fellow officer.

The engineer felt as if somebody had cut the deck out from beneath his feet. "But . . . what about my session . . . ?" he asked her.

Troi took him in tow as she headed for the door. "We'll continue as soon as we can," she said. "I promise."

Inwardly, he panicked. "But . . . I never got to tell you about my . . ."

The counselor stopped at the threshold. The doors to her quarters were already opening to let them out.

"Reg," she said, "I know that this isn't easy for you,

but try to relax. Getting yourself all keyed up isn't going to make things better."

"Try to relax," he echoed, focusing on the advice as she guided him out into the corridor. "That's a good idea." But deep down, he had a feeling it wouldn't work. Relaxing wasn't one of his strong points.

And a moment later, it was too late to remind her of the fact—because Troi was on her way into the turbolift opposite her quarters. As the lift doors closed, he was left standing in the middle of the hallway, watching as other crewmen went about their business.

Easy for *them* to face what was ahead, he thought. They weren't so petrified they could hardly breathe. Or stand up straight. Or *see*.

And it wasn't just that he was scared of dying. He suffered from another, more insidious fear . . . the nightmarish idea that he would freeze at a crucial moment and be responsible for others losing their lives. He was afraid that if the pressure got too great, he might make a gibbering, useless spectacle of himself.

In other words, he was frightened of being frightened. Terrified of being terrified. Paralyzed by the prospect of paralysis.

But maybe the counselor was right. Maybe all he had to do was relax. A holodeck program would . . .

He stopped himself. No, not the holodeck. He'd had his share of problems there.

Then the gym . . .

Again, he stopped short. He wasn't very physical. Going to the gym would only make him feel inadequate.

There was always that other place. Come to think of it, he was in the mood for one of Guinan's lime rickeys.

And she was always willing to listen to him, no matter how silly his concerns were.

His course set, he turned to the turbolift. After a wait of only a few seconds, the doors opened to admit him. But as he stepped inside, feeling he was taking the proper steps to solve his problem, he felt a flush crawl up his cheeks.

Wait a minute . . .

Why had the counselor been called away so abruptly? Could it be that something had happened . . . something related to the massing of Romulan ships along the Neutral Zone? Something really *bad?*

Had there been an attack? Were they at war *already?*

Before he could come to grips with the notion, the calm of the lift compartment was shattered by the urgent sound of a klaxon.

"Red alert," announced the ship's computer in a feminine voice. "This is not a drill. Red alert. This is not a drill . . ."

CHAPTER 14

Picard sat at the head of the table that dominated the observation lounge and surveyed his officers' faces. Their expressions ranged from concern to disbelief to resentment—all emotions he himself had experienced in Q's twenty-first-century courtroom.

Only Data remained nonplussed. But then, he was *always* like that—at least in *this* time frame.

"So?" the captain prodded. "What do you think?"

Geordi shook his head. "I don't believe him. This has to be another one of his games. He's probably listening to us right now, getting a big laugh out of watching us jump through his hoops."

"Nonetheless," commented Picard, "I think this time we have no choice but to take him at his word . . . which means that in some fashion, *I* will cause the destruction of humanity."

Beverly leaned forward. "But didn't Q say you already *had* caused it?"

Deanna nodded. "Yes . . . and that you were causing it even now?"

Riker sighed. "This is starting to give me a headache."

Data's brow creased ever so slightly. "Given the fact that there is an apparent discontinuity between the three time periods the captain is visiting, Q's statement may be accurate, if confusing. The actions that the captain has taken in the past have already occurred, while his actions here in the present are still transpiring . . ."

"And in the future," said Picard, completing the thought, "there are actions I have yet to undertake."

The android looked at him. "Exactly, sir."

Worf scowled. "Now *I* am getting a headache."

"So," asked the captain, "what should I do? Just lock myself in a room in all three time periods? Is that the only way I can avoid causing this . . . cataclysm?"

"It could also be your *inaction* that causes the destruction of mankind," Riker pointed out. "What if you were needed on the bridge at a key moment, and you weren't there?"

"We can't start second-guessing ourselves," advised Deanna. "There's no way to rationally predict what's going to happen. I think we have to proceed normally . . . deal with each situation as it occurs. Otherwise, we'll become paralyzed with indecision."

Picard nodded. "Agreed." He paused, pursuing another line of thought. "It would seem that there is some connection between my jumping through time . . . Q's threat . . . and the appearance of a spatial anomaly in the Neutral Zone. Speculation?"

"There are many possibilities," replied Data. "Your time shifts could be causing the spatial anomaly. Or it could be that the anomaly is causing your time shifts."

"But why the captain?" asked Worf. "Why does it seem to be only affecting him?"

That made them all stop and think. It was Picard himself who responded first—and with a conclusion that surprised even himself.

"There is another possibility. What if Q himself were endowing me with this time-shifting ability . . . in order to give me a chance to save humanity?"

There were astonished looks all around. "What makes you say that?" asked the first officer.

"Q has always shown a certain . . . fascination with humanity," the captain explained. "And more specifically, with me. I think he has more than a casual interest in what happens to me."

"That is true," agreed Data. "Q's interest in you is very similar to that of a master in a beloved pet. In a way, he may relate to you the way I relate to Spot."

Picard was less than thrilled with that comparison. He communicated that with a look.

The android tilted his head slightly. "It was only an analogy, Captain."

"Yes," remarked Picard. "And unfortunately, it's rather close to the truth. Let's assume for the moment that Q does regard me as a sort of . . . prized possession. He may not want to see that possession destroyed. And yet, he may be prohibited from acting directly to prevent it."

"You mean by the other Q?" asked Geordi.

"Yes. Or perhaps even by his own code of behavior," the captain suggested. "That is, if he has one we're not aware of."

"Maybe," said Riker, "he gave you this ability to shift through time so you could see a problem developing . . . at three different points."

The captain pondered that possibility. "A problem that can only be solved by marshaling the resources of three different time periods . . ."

His cogitation was cut short by a message over the intercom. "Ensign Calan to Captain Picard."

Picard looked up. "Go ahead, Ensign."

"We're approaching the Neutral Zone, sir."

The captain saw his officers exchange glances.

"On our way," he replied.

As they filed out onto the bridge, each of them moved to his or her customary place. Sitting down in his seat, Picard considered the starfield he saw on the viewscreen.

"All stop," he commanded. "Long-range scan."

It took a moment for his people to make the adjustment to the sensor array. And another for the results to come in.

"There are four Romulan Warbirds on the other side of the Neutral Zone," Data informed him from his position at ops. "They are holding position, sir. And on our side of the border, the Federation starships *Concord* and *Bozeman* are holding position as well."

"A standoff," remarked Riker. "The question is, who's going to move first?"

"We are," responded the captain. "Mr. Worf, hail the Romulan flagship. We have nothing to gain by maintaining an uneasy silence."

"Aye, sir," said the Klingon. And a moment later: "Her commander is responding."

"On screen," Picard told him . . .

. . . and the image of an aged Klingon supplanted the starfield.

Startled, Picard looked around for an explanation—and realized that he was no longer on the *Enterprise*. He was on the *Pasteur*, in what he had come to think of as the "future."

Beverly was seated beside him. He gripped the armrest of her chair as he adjusted to the sudden shift.

It took him another second or two to recognize the Klingon on the viewscreen as Worf. The former security officer was sitting at a desk in what looked like a small, crowded office. The furniture behind him was stacked high with books and documents.

"Captain Picard," said the governor, inclining his head as a peculiarly Klingon sign of respect.

Beverly nodded. "Hello, Worf. It's been a long time."

"That it has," the Klingon agreed. "I have read your request."

He paused, as if steeling himself for his next statement. That alone suggested to Picard that the news would not be good.

"The first thing you should know," he continued, "is that I am no longer a member of the High Council."

It was true. The news was *not* good. If Worf had fallen from favor, their job would be that much harder.

"After I opposed our withdrawal from the Federation Alliance," the Klingon explained, "the House of Mogh was forced from power. Exiled—albeit unofficially—from the homeworld."

"I see," said Beverly. She was obviously trying to be sympathetic.

But Picard didn't see. He didn't see at all. "Worf," he pleaded, "you must still have *some* influence. We need your help."

The Klingon scowled in self-derision. "I am only the governor of this colony." He spoke the words as if they constituted a curse. "My powers are . . . mostly ceremonial." Abruptly, a strain of anger crept into his voice. "If Admiral Riker had given you a starship with a cloak, you would have been safe. I cannot *believe* he refused to help you."

Picard held his hands out. "I don't care what kind of ship we're in—cloaked or otherwise. The important thing is to get to the Devron system." His hands balled into fists as he pleaded his case. "Surely . . . even with what's happened to you . . . it's within your power to grant us permission to cross the border. If nothing else, at least *that.*"

Worf looked down, then shook his shaggy head. "I am sorry, but my first duty is to the Empire. I must adhere to regulations."

The captain eyed him. He had to try a different approach.

"Maybe I'm an old man who just doesn't understand," he said. "But the Worf I knew cared more about things like loyalty and honor than he did about rules and regulations."

As he paused for effect, he saw the Klingon's head come up, so that he gazed at Picard from beneath his protruding brow. It seemed he had gotten Worf's attention.

"But then," he concluded, driving in the final stake, "that was a long time ago. Maybe you're not the Worf I knew."

He had expected to spur an emotional reaction—but he wasn't prepared for the actual violence of the governor's outburst. In a fit of untrammeled rage, Worf swept everything from his desk. Computer disks flew through the air like deadly weapons while official reports erupted in a storm of loose papers.

"Dor-sHo GHA!" the Klingon bellowed, trembling with fury. He brought his fist down on the desk like a sledgehammer, making it jump.

Indeed, thought Picard, holding his ground.

His eyes flashing with anger, Worf pointed an accusatory finger at his former captain. "You have always used your knowledge of Klingon honor and tradition to get what you want from me."

"That's right," Picard shot back, measure for measure. "Because it always works. Your problem, my friend, is that you really *do* have a sense of honor. You really care about things like loyalty and trust." He snorted. "Don't blame me because I know you too well, Worf. Blame yourself for embodying the virtues to which others only pretend."

The Klingon glared at him. His rage was cooling, by degrees.

"Very well," he snarled at last. "You may cross the border. But *only* if I come with you. No one is more familiar with the Neutral Zone than I am—and you will need a guide." He frowned. "There are those in the

Empire who long for battle with the Federation . . . who believe that we were taken advantage of during the years of the alliance. They will not hesitate to fire on an unauthorized vessel."

Picard smiled in his beard. This was more than he could have hoped for. "Terms accepted," he said.

A moment later, Worf's visage was replaced by a motionless starfield. The transmission was at an end.

And Picard had gotten what he wanted. They were on their way to the Devron system.

Beverly turned to Chilton. "Ensign," she said, "inform transporter room two that the governor is to be beamed aboard."

"Aye, sir," replied the conn officer.

As Worf came around his desk and waited for the transport, he reflected on what this decision would mean to his career. A Klingon didn't abandon his post—even if it was a purely bureaucratic one. No doubt, he'd be taken to task . . . perhaps even stripped of his title.

He grinned recklessly, for the first time in many years. Worse things could happen than losing a position he had never wanted in the first place. It was a good day to be dismissed, he mused.

Just then, one of his assistants entered the room with a padd in his hand. "Governor," he said, "I have the supply report for your—"

"K'dho moqak!" bellowed Worf.

His assistant took a couple of steps back, astonished at his superior's outburst. It was a second or two before he could bring himself to speak.

"But, Governor . . ."

"Cancel all of my appointments for the next few days," Worf instructed—then thought better of it. "No," he amended with some satisfaction. "Cancel all my appointments . . . *period.*"

His assistant shook his head. "I do not understand," he groaned. "The delegation from Krios . . ."

"Can solve its own, small-minded problems," Worf replied.

And before he had to put up with any further protests, he found himself somewhere else entirely. It took him a heartbeat to realize that he had materialized on one of the *Pasteur*'s transporter platforms.

"Welcome aboard," said the transporter operator—a slender Malcorian female with long red hair twisted into a braid.

He nodded. He was here. Whatever happened from this point on, he would acquit himself honorably.

CHAPTER **15**

Picard saw Chilton swivel to address Beverly. "Governor Worf is aboard," the woman reported.

Beverly nodded by way of acknowledgment. No doubt she was as glad to have Worf along as Picard himself was. On a jaunt like the one they were contemplating, he reflected, they could use all the help they could get.

Turning to him, Beverly waxed serious. "I just want to make one thing clear, Jean-Luc. If we run into any serious opposition, I'm taking us back to Federation territory. This isn't a Galaxy-class starship and we wouldn't last very long in a fight."

She was right, of course. There were reasonable limits to what they could accomplish—and were their situations reversed, he would have established that fact as she had.

But this was not any ordinary mission—and extraordinary missions sometimes called for extraordinary measures. Fortunately, that was something he could address later on. There was no reason to invite a confrontation with his ex-wife at this point.

He nodded, for the sake of peace. "I understand."

"All right," said Beverly, apparently satisfied. "Ensign, set course for the Devron system. Warp 13."

As Picard watched, she raised her hand to give the order to engage—then stopped and looked to him instead. Slowly, a wistful smile came to her. "Once more?" she suggested. "For old time's sake, Jean-Luc?"

He grinned, knowing exactly what she meant. As he had a thousand times on the *Enterprise,* he held up his hand in that old, familiar way.

"Engage," he said.

"Engage to where, sir?" O'Brien cast a querulous look at him.

But O'Brien wasn't on the *Pasteur.* And as the captain looked around, he saw that *he* wasn't, either.

He was back on the *Enterprise,* in the past. Taking a deep breath to steady himself, Picard studied the viewscreen. It showed him the sun and several planets that constituted the Chavez system.

But that was no longer his objective. Now that he'd learned a few things, he had another destination in mind.

"Set course for the Devron system," he instructed O'Brien, "and engage at warp nine."

Troi looked at him, concern evident in her dark eyes. "Sir, the Devron system is *inside* the Neutral Zone."

Tasha chimed in as well from her position at tactical. "We've received no orders to enter the Zone, sir."

The captain cast a withering glance at her. "I'm aware of that, Lieutenant. Carry out my orders, Chief."

O'Brien nodded. "Aye, sir."

Picard could tell that worried looks were being exchanged behind his back. He did his best to ignore them.

A moment later, Troi was at his side. "Captain," she said, in a voice too low for anyone else to hear it, "may I have a word with you in private?"

"Of course," replied Picard. Addressing Tasha again, he said, "Lieutenant, contact Farpoint Station. I want to speak with Commander Riker."

"Aye, sir," she responded. But she was obviously distracted by the impending conference between the captain and his ship's counselor.

Picard was pleased to note that, even at this early stage in their relationship, Troi was impeccably discreet. She waited until the ready-room doors had closed behind them before launching into a conversation.

"Captain," she said, "I just want to voice my concerns about the way the crew is responding to your . . . unexpected orders."

"They don't trust me," he acknowledged. "I know that. They think I'm behaving erratically."

Troi nodded. "Some do. Others are simply confused. It takes some time for a new crew to get to know their captain, and for him to know them."

"I understand that," he told her. "But I know what this crew is capable of, even if they don't. And I believe that they have the ability to become one of the finest crews in the fleet."

She smiled. "I'm happy to hear you say that. It may do *them* good to hear it, as well." A pause. "It would also help if they knew what was going on. In fact, it would help a lot."

Picard took a moment to consider his response. "I know it's difficult operating in the dark," he said finally. "But for now, I believe it's the only way."

Troi looked unconvinced. "Perhaps if you could at least indicate why you feel that—"

She was interrupted by Tasha's intercom voice. "Lieutenant Yar to Captain Picard. I have Commander Riker for you, sir."

Picard noticed the counselor's reaction to the mention of Riker's name. It told him that this was a woman who had not resolved her feelings about her former lover.

He looked up at the intercom grid in the ceiling. "Thank you, Lieutenant. Put Commander Riker through in here."

"Aye, sir."

The captain sat down at his desk and activated the desktop monitor. Instantly, the image of a young, beardless Will Riker sprang into view. Picard didn't look to see the expression on Troi's face, but he had a pretty good idea what it might be.

"Commander," he said. "I just wanted to let you know we won't be picking you up at Farpoint Station, as scheduled."

Riker seemed mildly disturbed. "I see. May I ask why?"

"Not at this time," the captain advised him.

His exec showed a little surprise, but he didn't act on it. "And how long do you expect to be delayed, sir?"

Picard shook his head. "I'm not sure at the moment. However, I'll keep you updated. Please inform Dr. Crusher and Lieutenant La Forge of our delay as well."

"Understood, sir."

And with that, the captain brought the transmission to an end.

At Farpoint Station, Beverly Crusher was just finishing breakfast when her door whistled. On a starship, visitors were announced with the sound of chimes, but the Bandi had naturally designed the place with their own preferences in mind.

"Come in," she said.

A moment later, the doors parted to reveal the rangy figure of Will Riker. He smiled in that easy way he had.

"Sorry to bother you," he said.

"That's quite all right," Crusher told him. She was, of course, already acquainted with the first officer from her passage here on the *Hood*. He had been an exec there too, under Captain DeSoto.

"Mom? Is that Commander Riker?"

Before she could answer, her son Wesley rushed in from his bedroom. His dark eyes were wide with delight —and no wonder. The commander had been good enough to take Wesley under his wing on the *Hood,* patiently answering the boy's multitudinous questions about starship operating systems.

"Yes," she replied, just for the record. "It's Commander Riker, all right."

The man's smile widened. "How goes it, Wes?"

Her son shrugged his narrow shoulders. "Not bad. I

was just reading up on the new plasma conduits they've been installing on all the newer vessels." He paused, so beset with curiosity that he was almost in pain. "If I ask nicely, do you think the captain will let me see them?"

It was Riker's turn to shrug. "I can't say for sure, Wes. I've never met him, so I don't know what he's like. But I'll put in a good word for you."

Wesley's pain seemed to dissipate. "Great," he said hopefully. Then he turned to Crusher herself. "Mom, could you put in a good word for me too?"

Riker looked at her, a question on his face. The doctor could feel the rush of blood to her cheeks.

"Captain Picard and my late husband were friends," she explained concisely. "I guess I never mentioned that, did I?"

The first officer shook his head. "No, ma'am, you didn't. But under the circumstances, maybe you could put in a good word for *both* of us."

Coming from someone else, it might have sounded sarcastic, even resentful. When Riker said it, it made her laugh. Whatever embarrassment she had felt was instantly gone.

She wished she could feel that good about joining the crew of the *Enterprise*. Truth to tell, she hadn't selected this assignment with the express purpose of serving with her husband's old friend. Quite the contrary; she had had to think twice about it before signing on.

After all, Jack had died a decade ago—while under Picard's command. The last time she had seen the captain was at her husband's funeral.

Their working together now, on the same ship, would be awkward, to say the least. She would be an uncomfortable reminder of a colleague's death—for which he couldn't help but blame himself, however unfairly. And he would be a symbol of what Jack might have become, if he hadn't perished in that awful accident.

Still, she had wanted this position. After all her training, all she'd accomplished in the medical corps, it was the only real challenge left to her. And Beverly Crusher had never been one to back down from a challenge.

"I'll do what I can," she told Commander Riker.

"Unfortunately," the first officer said, his smile fading a little, "I think we're going to have to wait a little longer before we can put in those good words of ours. I've just spoken with Captain Picard, and he tells me our rendez-vous has been postponed . . . indefinitely."

The doctor saw the disappointment on her son's face. "Why?" he asked. It was a logical question.

"I wish I could say," Riker responded. "However, the captain didn't see fit to tell me."

Now Crusher *did* hear a note of resentment in the man's voice. Apparently, Will Riker didn't like to be left out of things. At least, not when they pertained to his ship and his commanding officer.

Wesley plunked himself down on a nearby couch. "I *knew* this was too good to be true," he sighed.

The first officer placed a hand on the boy's shoulder. "Whatever called the captain away," he advised, "it'll probably only mean another day or two. You can hold out *that* long, can't you?"

Looking up, Wesley nodded. "I guess so," he answered.

Riker nodded. "Good." He turned to the doctor. "In

that case, I'll be heading over to Lieutenant La Forge's quarters. I could tell him over station intercom," he noted, "but I think I'll do it in person. Lord knows, I've got all the time in the world."

Crusher chuckled. Wasn't *that* the truth.

On the *Enterprise,* the captain turned again to Troi. "Is there anything else, Counselor?"

She didn't answer right away. Clearly, something was troubling her.

"Actually," she said, "there is, sir. I've been debating whether or not to mention it, but perhaps . . ." She became more resolute. "It's about Commander Riker."

Picard, of course, knew all about their relationship back on Betazed. He even knew how it would run its course in the future. But, unable to reveal anything of events to come, he played it as if this was the first he had heard of it.

"What about him?" he asked.

"Well," Troi began, "I think you should know that we . . . have had a prior relationship."

The captain looked at her, feigning surprise. "I see. And do you anticipate this interfering with your duties?"

She shook her head fervently. "No, sir. It was many years ago—and I'm sure it's well behind us both. I just thought you should know."

Picard pretended to ponder the information—and then to come to a decision. "I appreciate your telling me, Counselor. However, I'm sure the two of you will find a way to . . . deal with the situation."

Troi nodded . . . though she didn't seem as certain as he was. Moving to the replicator in the room, the captain requested his beverage of choice.

"Tea. Earl Grey. Hot."

The computer's response was instantaneous—and a little unnerving. "That beverage has not been programmed into this station. Please enter chemical composition."

Picard smiled. As he turned to Troi, intending to cover his surprise with a clever remark . . .

. . . he found himself standing in front of the ship's viewscreen—and the image of the Romulan commander that filled it.

It took him a second or two to get his bearings . . . to establish that he was back in the "present." And another second to realize that he recognized the Romulan.

"Tomalak," he whispered.

He had run into the Romulan before—first at Galorndon Core, then when Picard had granted asylum to Admiral Jarok. Tomalak looked every bit as formidable as on those previous occasions.

"So, Captain," said the craggy-faced Romulan. "How long shall we stare at each other across the Neutral Zone?"

Gathering himself, Picard returned the scrutiny. How long indeed? Then he got an idea.

"There is an alternative, you know."

"And what is that?" asked Tomalak.

The captain shrugged. "It's obvious that we're both

here for the same reason—to find out more about the anomaly in the Devron system."

"All right," the Romulan concurred. "What do you propose?"

"Simply this," said Picard. "We could each send one ship into the Neutral Zone—with the sole purpose of investigating the anomaly."

Tomalak considered the plan. "Has Starfleet Command approved this arrangement?"

It hadn't, of course. "No," the captain replied honestly.

The Romulan smiled. "I like it already."

His eyes narrowed as he weighed the proposition in greater detail, inspecting it from all angles. At last, he nodded.

"It is agreed. One ship from each side. But I warn you—if another Federation starship tries to enter the Zone . . ."

"You needn't make threats," said Picard. "I think we're all aware of the consequences."

"Very well," replied Tomalak, almost amiably. "See you in the Devron system, Captain."

A moment later, the Romulan was gone, replaced by a static starfield full of Neutral Zone constellations.

Picard turned to the officer who was sitting at conn. "Set course for the Devron system, Ensign. Warp five . . . *engage.*"

CHAPTER 16

Guinan had expected that the captain would come calling on her at any moment. She wasn't disappointed.

Even as he entered Ten-Forward, he was scanning the place. Scanning it for *her*. Of course, she wasn't at her usual spot behind the bar, so it took him a moment to find her.

"Excuse me," she told Reg Barclay, as she got up from their table. "I've got a prior engagement."

The engineer turned pale. "But . . . I mean . . ."

"I know," Guinan told him, placing a reassuring hand on his shoulder. "You need to talk to someone. You're scared about what's going on. But so is everyone else." She looked into his eyes. "It's all right to be scared, Mr. Barclay. It doesn't mean there's something wrong with you. It means there's something *right.*"

His forehead wrinkled. "You . . . you really think so?"

"I *know* so. And I also know that you've always come

through in a pinch—no matter how much you worried about it beforehand."

Barclay thought about it. "I guess . . . you're right," he told her.

She grinned. "So what else is new?" Then, giving him a last pat, she beckoned her top waiter. As Ben approached, she said, "Another lime rickey for our Mr. Barclay. And don't hold back on the grenadine."

Ben nodded. "Gotcha," he said, and headed back to the bar.

By then, Picard was standing in the center of the room, waiting for her. As Guinan approached him, she smiled.

"Come here often?" she asked.

He almost smiled back. "Not as often as I'd prefer," he admitted. "Of course, this isn't just a friendly visit."

Guinan nodded. "Care to step into my office?"

"In fact," he said, "I would like that."

Taking his arm, she guided him to a secluded spot near one of the observation ports. From there, they could see the stars rushing by.

As they sat, a waiter started in their direction. However, Guinan waved him away before he got very far. Acknowledging her signal, the man veered off in a different direction.

"I'm assuming," she said, as she turned back to the captain, "that you're not very thirsty."

"Your assumption is correct," he told her. Then he paused, as he gathered his thoughts. "Guinan, I have a problem. A rather large problem. And I was hoping you could help me with it."

"It has to do with this time-skipping business," she commented. It wasn't a question.

Picard regarded her with narrowed eyes. "Then you've heard . . . ?"

She nodded. "You're not surprised, are you?"

After a moment, the captain shook his head. "No, I suppose not. Or at least, I shouldn't be." He leaned forward, his features softened by the lounge's strategic lighting. "Guinan, I have had a conversation with a mutual friend of ours . . ."

"Q," she clarified. The very sound was distasteful to her.

"Yes. He has informed me that I will cause the destruction of all humanity. What's more, this will take place in three distinct time periods—but in each one, I will be at the root of it."

"I see," she replied.

"Now," he went on, "we have discovered a spatial anomaly in the Devron system, for which we are headed even as we speak. I believe this anomaly may be the cause of the destruction that Q spoke of . . ."

"But you can't be certain," she clarified. "For all you know, the anomaly has nothing to do with it whatsoever."

"That's correct," he confirmed. "Likewise, it appears to me that Q may be the one responsible for my time-shifting . . . though again, I have no proof. And if he *is* responsible, I cannot say if his intentions are benign or malevolent. After all, my travel through time may be what creates the problem—or what enables me to solve it. I have no way of knowing."

Guinan shook her head in sympathy. "You've got a lot of gaps to fill, haven't you?"

"I have," Picard agreed. "Which is where I hope you will come in. After all, you were the only one who retained some sense of perspective when the *Enterprise* fell victim to that temporal rift. . . ."

"I remember," she replied. "The one in which we switched timelines . . . and found ourselves at war with the Klingons. The one in which Tasha Yar was still alive."

He nodded. "Yes. And what's more, you know Q better than any of us. You make him uncomfortable . . . even fearful, I think. Now, I'm just guessing, but I believe you are capable of straightening out this mess. If not directly, then at least indirectly—by giving me the insight I need to set matters right on my own."

Guinan looked at him. She would have liked nothing better than to fulfill her friend's request. However . . .

"I'm afraid that's not possible," she said.

The captain couldn't conceal his disappointment. "Are you saying that you *can't* help? Or you *won't?*"

"What I'm saying," she explained, choosing her words carefully, "is that you're on your own this time, Jean-Luc. And that's *all* I can say."

He leaned back in his chair. "You understand how much is at stake here? How much we stand to lose?"

"I have a pretty good idea," she responded.

"And that doesn't change anything?" he pressed.

"I wish it did," said Guinan. "And I wish I could make it clear why it doesn't. But . . ." She shrugged.

Picard tried to accept her answer. "Then there's

nothing you can tell me that could be of help to me? Nothing at all?"

She thought for a moment. "Only," she responded at last, "that the solution is within your grasp. And that only you can do the grasping."

The captain took a breath and let it out. Obviously, it wasn't what he had hoped for. But it was *something*.

"Thank you," he said sincerely, "if only for that."

Guinan smiled ironically. "That's what I'm here for."

"It almost doesn't *matter* why we're here," remarked Ensign Sonya Gomez, checking the warp drive's power-transfer ratios on her monitor down in engineering.

"Doesn't matter?" echoed Ensign Robin Lefler, who was standing next to her. It was Lefler's job to examine the dilithium crystal for tiny plasma chinks—a routine job made just a little less routine by the ship's current location and heading. "You're not just a little concerned about what's going on here at the Neutral Zone?" she asked.

"Sure I am," responded Gomez. "But think of it . . . we're in the *Neutral Zone*. We're looking at star systems that haven't been seen since the Treaty of Algeron—at least, not with the naked eye."

Lefler smiled at her. "Or rather, we *would* be . . . if there were any observation ports here in engineering. Maybe they're seeing those places up in Ten-Forward— but down here, all we've got are our sensor reports."

Gomez frowned. "Okay, so we're not actually *seeing* them. But still, it's exciting knowing that they're out there. And that we're among them." She paused. "Some of the greatest captains that ever lived haven't been inside the Neutral Zone."

Lefler shrugged. "I suppose."

Gomez turned to her. "But you're still not excited?"

Her colleague sighed. "Sure I am. But I can't help thinking about rule number twenty-nine."

"Rule number twenty-nine?" repeated Gomez. "What's that?"

"The sightseeing's just as good on the way home," replied Lefler. Her brow creased as she scrutinized her monitor a little more closely.

Gomez regarded her. "What does that mean?"

Without looking up, Lefler patted her on the shoulder. "It means pay attention to those power-transfer ratios— or we might not *get* home."

"Oh," said Gomez. And, reflecting on the wisdom of rule number twenty-nine, she put her thoughts of undiscovered star systems aside.

At least, for the time being.

It hadn't taken long to reach the Devron system, Picard reflected, as he considered the viewscreen from his captain's chair. Or, for that matter, to discover that there was something there well worth the trip.

Data swiveled in his chair. "According to our sensors, we have located the anomaly."

Geordi whistled from his engineering station. "I've never seen anything like *that*," he commented.

"Nor have I," agreed Worf.

"It's beautiful," observed Deanna.

"So's a Venus's-flytrap," Riker reminded them.

It was just as the long-range scan reports had described it—a riotous blaze of color, pierced through with shafts of silver light. On the screen, the phenomenon had an ethereal quality to it, rendering it both spectacular and frightening all at once.

Getting up from his chair, Picard took a few steps toward it. He could almost feel it staring back at him, challenging him to unravel its secrets before it was too late.

He turned to Data, who was sitting at ops. "Full scan," he said.

"Aye, sir," the android replied, and set to work.

As the captain watched Data's fingers fly over his controls . . .

. . . he had the strangest feeling that he had made another time shift. A quick look around confirmed it. If Tasha was at tactical, he was back in the past.

Data turned to glance back over his shoulder at Picard. "We are approaching the Devron system, Captain. Sensors are picking up a large subspace anomaly directly ahead."

Picard grunted softly. Where had he heard that before?

"All stop. Put it on screen," he commanded.

As before, the viewscreen showed him the conflagration of temporal energies that composed the spatial anomaly. This time, however, it took up a good deal more of the screen.

Without meaning to, the captain said, "It's bigger, isn't it?"

Troi looked at him. "Sir?"

Picard shook his head. "Nothing. Full scan, Mr. Data."

"Aye, sir."

Taking a couple of steps forward, the captain peered at the screen, where the anomaly . . .

. . . was gone!

Picard blinked, but he couldn't make the thing come back. Instead, the viewscreen displayed a single yellow sun and three lifeless, nondescript planets.

Even before he surveyed his surroundings, he knew that he was in the future again. It was the only one of the three time frames in which his thoughts were so muddled, his brain so unresponsive.

"I've made a complete scan of the Devron system," said Data. "Sensors show nothing out of the ordinary."

Picard turned and saw that the android was at an aft console, working with La Forge as Worf looked on. The Klingon was shaking his shaggy head.

"No," said the captain. "That can't be."

He walked aft to join them; his heart was thudding against his ribs. Surely, they had made some mistake.

"I've already seen it in the other two . . . the other two time periods," he protested. "There should be a . . . a huge spatial anomaly here."

Geordi looked up. "I'm sorry, sir, but we've checked everything. There's just nothing here."

That wasn't right. It had to be here, thought Picard. It *had* to be.

155

CHAPTER **17**

It wasn't the result Beverly had hoped for. As she stood there with the others at the science station, her heart went out to Jean-Luc.

He had been so *sure* that they would find something out here. She had even begun to wonder if he might not be right—if all this business about time travel and mankind's destruction might not have had some tenuous basis in fact.

However, the evidence was undeniable. There was nothing to be seen here, nothing at all. She could only imagine his disappointment.

"Check again," Jean-Luc insisted.

Data did as he was asked. It didn't change a thing.

"Still nothing, Captain. I've conducted a full sensor sweep out to one light-year from the *Pasteur*. No temporal anomalies . . . or anything even resembling one."

"Have you scanned the subspace bandwidth?" asked Jean-Luc, stubbornly resisting reality.

"Yes, sir," replied Geordi. "The subspace barrier is a little thin in this region of space . . ."

"Ah-hah!" the older man cried.

Geordi frowned. "But, as I was about to say, sir, that's not unusual. In other words, we still haven't got anything to hang our hat on."

Jean-Luc's celebration died aborning. He shook his head.

"I don't understand. I've already seen it in the other two . . . the other two time periods. Why isn't it here?"

Worf, who had been working at a neighboring console, suddenly looked up with concern. "Captain," he said, his eyes fixing on Beverly. "I have been monitoring Klingon communication channels—and several warships have been dispatched to this sector. They are searching for a . . . renegade Federation vessel."

Damn, thought Beverly. The jig was up. It was time to get out of here—assuming there *was* still time.

Her ex-husband tugged on her sleeve. "You're not thinking about leaving, are you?"

She sighed, not wanting to hurt his feelings any more than they'd already been hurt. But there was no other way.

"Jean-Luc," she said, "there's nothing here. . . ."

"There should be!" he roared. "There *has* to be!"

Turning to Data, he leaned over and grabbed him by the shoulders. He'd relied on the android so many times in the past, he obviously didn't know how to stop.

"There must be some other way to scan for temporal disturbances," Jean-Luc cajoled. "Something that's not covered in a normal sensor sweep . . ."

Data considered the suggestion. "There are several

methods of detecting temporal disturbances," he noted, "but we are limited by the range of equipment on the *Pasteur*. This ship is designed primarily for medical emergencies, not scientific research."

Beverly interposed herself between the two of them. "Jean-Luc," she explained, "we've done all we can. We have to head back to Federation territory."

"However," Data went on, unperturbed, "it may be possible to modify the warp deflector to emit an inverse tachyon pulse, which could scan beyond the subspace barrier."

That changed Jean-Luc's demeanor again. All of a sudden, he was shaking his fists in the air in front of him.

"Very good!" he exclaimed. "Make it so!"

"Wait a minute," Beverly interjected. Turning to the android, she asked, "How long would this take?"

He shrugged. "To make the modifications and search the entire Devron system will take approximately fourteen hours."

She grunted. "Worf, how long until those Klingon warships get here?"

The Klingon sighed. "I am uncertain—but I believe they are coming from the Memp'ha Outpost. That would put them anywhere from eight to eleven hours away."

Time wasn't on their side, was it? Under the circumstances, she'd have to be crazy to pursue this thing any further—even if Data did give Jean-Luc's theory some credence.

But then, she'd done crazy things before.

"All right, Data. Begin modifying the tachyon pulse. Ensign Chilton, lay in a course back to the Federation. If we haven't found anything in six hours, we're heading back at maximum warp."

Chilton nodded. "Aye, sir."

"Six hours aren't enough," Jean-Luc protested. "We have to stay here until we find it—no matter how long it takes!"

Beverly felt something boil up inside her. It was all she could do to contain it.

"Carry out my orders," she told the ensign. And then, to Jean-Luc, she said tautly, "May I see you for a moment?"

His eyes were steely, full of righteous anger. "I should say so," he told her.

Without another word, she led him into her ready room.

As the doors closed behind them, Picard was still bristling with indignation. "Beverly," he said, "I can't believe you're not willing to stay here until—"

Abruptly, she whirled on him, her face flushed with anger. "Don't you *ever* question my orders on the bridge of my ship again!" she rasped.

He was caught completely off his guard. But in the next moment, he blustered back at her.

"I'm just trying to . . . There are larger concerns here than . . . Dammit, don't you understand that—"

"I understand," said Beverly, "that you would never have tolerated that kind of behavior back on the *Enterprise*. And I won't here."

Frustrated as he was, he had to concede that she had a point there. He would *not* have tolerated the kind of outburst he'd made on the bridge. He'd have sent the offender to his quarters to cool off. No—to the brig.

"You're right," he told her, chastened. "I was out of line. It won't happen again. But you have to understand . . . the stakes here are enormous. Q has assured me that all of humanity will be destroyed. . . ."

"I know," she answered. "And that's why I'm willing to stay here a while longer and keep looking." Her features softened, the fury dimming in her eyes. "But I also want you to consider the possibility that *none* of what you're saying is *real."*

It was like a slap in the face. He took a step backward.

"What are you saying . . . ?" he stammered.

Beverly moved toward him. She took his hands in hers.

"Jean-Luc, I care for you too much not to tell you the truth. You have advanced Irumodic syndrome. I have to weigh the possibility that all of this . . . the anomaly, the threat to mankind, everything . . . is in your mind." She paused. "I'll stay here for another six hours . . . and that's it. Then we're heading home."

He started to say something, but she gave him a look that told him she wouldn't argue the matter. And this time, he accepted it.

"I want you to remember something," Beverly said. "If it were anyone but you . . . anyone at all . . . I wouldn't have come here in the first place. I wouldn't even have considered it."

He believed her. Releasing his hands, she left him in the room to simmer down and returned to her bridge.

Alone, Picard mulled the whole thing over—and knew that his ex-wife had spoken the truth. He had pushed her . . . pushed all of his old friends . . . about as far as he could. And out of friendship, out of loyalty, they had acceded to his demands. But he could push them no further.

Suddenly, he got the sense that he was no longer by himself. There was someone in back of him.

Whirling, he saw what looked like a parody of an elderly man—someone with bags under his eyes, a mop of scraggly gray hair, and baggy, ill-fitting clothes. The grizzled old fellow was leaning on a cane and holding a hearing trumpet to one ear.

And, of course, it wasn't just any old buzzard who had materialized uninvited on the *Pasteur*. It was *Q*.

"Eh?" he croaked, in an exaggeration of the captain's voice. "What was that she said, sonny? I couldn't quite hear her. . . ."

Picard scowled. "What's going on here, Q? What have you done with the blasted anomaly?"

The old crow leaned closer to him, as if to hear better. "What's that? Where's your *mommy?* I don't know, sonny . . . where did you leave her?"

The captain's anger rose hot and red. "Stop this foolishness and answer me!" he bellowed, his voice cracking almost as badly as his adversary's.

Q wagged a spindly, arthritic finger at him. "You young whippersnappers are so impatient . . . always wanting answers. Why don't you just slow down . . . smell the roses . . . learn to appreciate the finer things in life . . ."

Picard took an angry step toward his nemesis—who, with a quickness that belied his elderly condition, raised his cane and planted the tip of it in the center of the human's chest. In that moment, Q's manner became markedly less playful.

"Now," he said, "don't get carried away, my ancient friend. You'll give yourself a heart attack. And I wouldn't want you to shuffle off before your time . . . which should be very soon, in any case."

"Not if I have any say in it!" the captain raged.

The entity peered into Picard's left eye. "Is that a blood clot in there, or are you just glad to see me?"

The captain fought down his fury. "Just tell me one thing, all right? This anomaly we're looking for . . . is this what destroys humanity?"

Q smiled a hideously wrinkled smile. "You're forgetting, Jean-Luc. I said *you* destroyed humanity."

"By doing what?" pressed Picard.

"That's for me to know," said the entity, "and you to find out. I thought I made that clear already."

The human swore. "When will this take place? How are you—"

Suddenly, he was no longer on the *Pasteur,* no longer in the future. He was back in the present, on the bridge of the *Enterprise.* The anomaly was on the viewscreen. And Q was nowhere to be seen.

On the other hand, the onmipotent trickster had left him a going-away present—the cane he'd been leaning on in Beverly's ready room. Tossing it aside, Picard walked forward to ops.

"Report, Mr. Data."

The android consulted the monitors on his console.

"The anomaly is two hundred million kilometers in diameter, sir. It is a highly focused temporal energy source which is emitting approximately the same energy output as ten G-type stars."

The captain considered the information. "And what is the source of that energy?"

"I am uncertain," replied Data. "Sensors have been unable to penetrate the anomaly."

Picard thought for a moment. In the future frame, the android had suggested that they . . .

"Data . . . what if we modified the warp deflector to emit an . . . inverse tachyon pulse? That might scan beyond the subspace barrier . . . and give us an idea what the interior of this thing looks like."

The android seemed a little surprised, but he considered it. "That is a most intriguing idea," he concluded. "I do not believe a tachyon beam has ever been put to such use." He paused. "What is more, I had no idea you were so versed in the intricacies of temporal theory."

The captain smiled at the irony. "I am not—but I have some friends who are. Make it so, Mr. Data."

"Aye, sir." He stood up from his place at ops. "I believe we can make the necessary modifications in main engineering."

Picard nodded. As Data headed for the turbolift, the captain turned back to the viewscreen. The anomaly roiled on, a symbol of annihilation that he didn't yet understand. However, he was determined that he *would*.

"A gift from a friend?" asked Riker. He was standing beside the captain with the discarded cane in his hands.

Picard glared at it. "Yes," he said. "A very *old* friend."

* * *

As Ensign Calan sat at her conn station, with little to do except watch the anomaly shimmer and burn on the viewscreen, her thoughts drifted back to an earlier time. She couldn't help it. When one had been through what she'd been through, it was difficult to leave it behind.

Like Ensigns Ro and Sito before her, Calan was a Bajoran. And like all Bajorans, she had been through hell at the hands of the Cardassians who had held her homeworld in thrall.

One memory in particular separated itself from the rest. It harkened back to the initial phase of the Cardassian occupation, when the worst atrocities were visited on her captive people.

Back then, Calan had labored in the kitchen of the Marjono prison camp—one of the larger facilities of its kind. Of course, the conqueror race had had no compunctions about putting children to work. In fact, they seemed to take satisfaction in it, as a sign of how thoroughly they had subjugated the Bajorans.

Little did they know how grateful she was for the job—because after the Cardassians had eaten their meal, it was her assignment to gather the dishes and bring them in for cleaning. And if she was quick about it, she could slip a crust of bread or a *jenka* root into her shirt, and share it with her fellow prisoners later on.

It wasn't as if Calan wasn't scared of retribution in those days; she was as scared as anyone else. But sometimes, hunger outweighed fear. What's more, it made her feel good to know she was striking back against the Cardassians in her own, small way.

If she had been older, she would have known that it was only a matter of time before she was caught. She would have predicted it as a certainty. But being a child, she didn't see it coming—and, perhaps reluctant to cut off their clandestine food supply, none of the others warned her about it.

But one day, when she was clearing the remains of a Cardassian's meal into her clothing, one of the guards saw what she was doing. Without a word, he grabbed her by her long blond hair and took her to the commandant of the prison camp.

Like so many Cardassians in high positions, Gul Makur was not an especially bad-tempered individual. However, he wasn't about to let Calan's audacity go unpunished. If his prisoners began to think they could get away with small things, he explained, they would try bigger things. And that would lead to the sort of trouble he'd prefer to avoid.

So to prevent small things from leading to bigger ones, the commandant took his dinner knife and dug it into the tender flesh of Calan's shoulder. He did this three times, until her shoulder bled in three spots. Then he connected the spots with the edge of his blade, creating a triangular scar that would remain with her the rest of her days.

Her only satisfaction came years later, when she heard that the Resistance had dispatched Gul Makur in a particularly slow and painful way. Then, in her mind, her scar became a badge of honor.

Even after she joined Starfleet and was given the option of having it surgically removed, she opted to keep it. It had become a part of her, and not the worst part by far.

As she often did when she remembered these events,

Calan reached beneath her uniform and felt for the raised triangle of the scar. Funny . . . for some reason, it was difficult to find. She felt around some more, but still came up empty-handed.

Ice water tricked down into the small of her back. It wasn't possible that the scar had disappeared. By the prophets, she had seen it this morning in the mirror. . . .

But after another moment or two, she came to a conclusion as inescapable as the Marjono prison camp. Her scar was gone, as if Gul Makur had never inflicted it on her in the first place.

Yet it hadn't been a dream; the damned thing had happened. Even now, she could feel the Cardassian's knife piercing her skin. She could feel the pain, the shame of her tears as they made hot little trails down her cheeks. . . .

No, the scar had been real. And now it was gone. The only question now was . . . *how?*

CHAPTER 18

"I'm surprised," said Geordi. "I had no idea that Captain Picard had such a handle on temporal theory."

"I was surprised as well," Data admitted, his voice only slightly masked by the hum of the engines.

They were working alongside each other in engineering, making the adjustments the captain had called for. Once the android had described what he was up to, Geordi couldn't resist pitching in. After all, he'd never even seen an inverse tachyon pulse, much less created one.

"And using the beam to scan past the subspace barrier . . ." The engineer shook his head. "That's pretty innovative . . . if it works."

"I thought so too," agreed Data.

"But," Geordi added, "I guess this isn't the first time Captain Picard has caught me off guard. It's amazing some of the things he comes up with."

The android nodded. "I suppose it is."

The engineer pointed to one of the monitors they were working with—and, more specifically, to a key juncture in the deflector schematic. "We can get more power if we reroute this circuit to the deflector array."

It seemed to make sense to Data also. "Initiating tachyon pulse . . ."

On another monitor, the engineer could see a thin, oscillating beam emerge from the deflector dish and begin scanning the anomaly.

After a moment, the android turned to him. "I am curious, Geordi. Where do you think you will be twenty-five years from now?"

The human smiled. "What?"

"Captain Picard has been to the future," Data explained. "All our futures. He might even be interacting with one or more of us in that time period. I find it interesting to speculate where our lives will take us by that time."

Geordi shrugged. "I don't know. Assuming I'm still around, I'll probably still be in Starfleet."

His friend looked at him. "Then you do not anticipate any significant changes in your future?"

The engineer shook his head. "Not really. I'm a pretty lucky guy. I'm doing exactly what I want in exactly the way I want to do it. I'll probably be wearing this uniform until the day I die." He paused. "What about you?"

Data thought for a moment. "I have often considered leaving Starfleet for academic study."

"So you'd like to teach?" Geordi asked.

"Possibly," Data answered. "My first choice would be to do so at Cambridge University. In an ideal situation, I would hold the Lucasian Chair, which was also held by

Sir Isaac Newton, Dr. Stephen Hawking, and Torar Olaffok." He seemed to hesitate. "But that is only a possibility. Perhaps I will remain in Starfleet as well."

It was time to check their instruments. "Okay," said Geordi. "The pulse is holding steady. We're starting to receive data from the scan. . . ."

"It will take the computer some time to give us a complete picture of the anomaly's interior," the android pointed out. "I suggest we——"

Before Data could finish his thought, Geordi felt a sudden stab of pain in both his eyes. "Damn!" he groaned, dropping his face into his hands.

"What is wrong?" asked Data.

"I'm not sure . . ." answered the engineer. He just knew it hurt like hell—and he'd never felt this kind of pain before. "It's like somebody put an ice pick through my temples . . . and my VISOR . . . it's picking up all kinds of electromagnetic distortions. . . ."

He staggered, lost his balance . . . and felt the android catch him before he could fall. The next thing he knew, his friend was speaking to the intercom system.

"Data to sickbay. Medical emergency in main engineering . . ."

Picard shook his head. He'd had his hands full wrestling with Q, his time shifts, and humanity's survival. Now something *else* seemed to be rearing its ugly head.

As he looked on, Beverly pointed to Geordi's eyes. The engineer was sitting on a biobed with his VISOR off.

"Look at them," said the doctor. "You can see the difference yourself."

It was true. Whereas Geordi's eyes had previously been perfectly colorless, they now showed signs of having irises. The signs were faint, but they were there.

"Yes," Picard responded. "I see."

Picking up a scanning device, Beverly used it to perform a quick examination. As she looked at the results, her forehead wrinkled.

"What is it?" the captain asked.

"Nothing short of amazing," she told him, still staring at the device. "The DNA in his optic nerves is being regenerated. I'm starting to see the formation of a *retina.*" She turned to Picard. "It's as if he were growing brand-new eyes."

Geordi swore beneath his breath. "I guess that's why I started to feel pain. My optical cortex was falling out of alignment with my VISOR."

Picard didn't understand. "How is this possible?" he asked.

"It shouldn't be possible at all," returned the chief medical officer. "There's no medical explanation for a spontaneous regeneration of dead tissue."

As they pondered her remark, Nurse Ogawa approached them. She held out a padd to Beverly.

"Doctor," said Ogawa, "we've just gotten reports from two crew members . . . Ensign Calan, and Lieutenant McBurney in astrophysics . . . who say they have old injuries that are healing themselves. I'm not sure what to make of it."

The captain looked at her. "Healing . . . themselves?" he echoed.

Before they could go any further, Data approached them. He had been working at a terminal off to the side—and in his fascination with Geordi's condition, Picard had all but forgotten that the android was there.

"I believe," said Data, "that I may have a partial explanation for what is happening to Commander La Forge . . . and to the others as well, sir. If you would care to join me, I can show you what I mean."

The captain and Beverly followed the android back to his terminal. Looking over Data's shoulder at the monitor, Picard could see a rather complex diagram of the anomaly with various pieces of sensor information incorporated into it. He waited for an explanation—nor was it long in coming.

"I have completed my analysis of the anomaly," said the android. "It appears to be a multiphasic temporal convergence in the space-time continuum."

The doctor frowned. "In English, please."

"It is, in essence," amended Data, "an eruption of *anti-time.*"

The captain looked at him. "Anti-time?"

"Yes, sir," confirmed the android. "It is a relatively new concept in temporal mechanics. The relationship of anti-time to normal time is analogous to the relationship of antimatter to normal matter."

Picard mulled that over. "All right," he said. "Go on."

"Anti-time," Data explained, "would possess the exact opposite characteristics of normal time—operating in some kind of temporal reversion we do not fully understand."

The captain was beginning to catch on. "You're saying that the anomaly is the result of time and anti-time coming together in the same place."

"That is correct, sir. Something has ruptured the

barrier between time and anti-time in the Devron system. I believe this rupture is sending out waves of temporal energy which are disrupting the normal flow of time."

The android turned to gaze at Geordi. "It is possible that the DNA molecules in Geordi's optic nerves are not regenerating themselves . . . but simply reverting to their original state."

If Data was right . . .

"You mean his eyes are getting *younger?*" asked Picard.

The android nodded. "For all intents and purposes, yes."

The captain considered the implications. "So the temporal anomaly has certain rejuvenating effects. It certainly doesn't sound like the destruction of humanity."

"No," Beverly confirmed. "It doesn't."

Picard scowled. "Mr. Data . . . any idea what could have caused this rupture between time and anti-time?"

Data looked confused. "Anti-time, sir?"

Abruptly, Picard realized that the android was sitting at ops, not at a terminal in sickbay. He gathered that he had returned to the past.

This was an opportunity, then. Moving quickly to Data's console, he began entering information as quickly as he could. The others—Tasha, Worf, O'Brien, and Troi—were no doubt watching from their stations, wondering what in blazes the captain was up to.

"I believe," he explained to the android, "that if we

modify the deflector to send out an inverse tachyon pulse, you'll find that the anomaly is a rupture between time and anti-time."

Data regarded him. "That is a fascinating hypothesis, sir. Where did you encounter—"

"It would take too long to explain," Picard told him. "Begin the modifications and send out the pulse. And once you've done that, start working on a theory as to what could have caused this rupture."

The android didn't question his motives. "Aye, sir."

As Data began to comply with his orders, the captain took in the image of the anomaly on the viewscreen. In case he had forgotten, he was reminded of how much larger it was here in the past than in the present.

"Mr. O'Brien," he said. "How big is the anomaly?"

It took only a moment or two for O'Brien to come up with the answer. "Approximately four hundred million kilometers in diameter, sir."

Picard shook his head, wishing he had a better grasp of what was going on. "I still don't understand why it's larger *here*. . . ."

O'Brien shot him a puzzled look. Obviously, he didn't have any idea what his commanding officer was talking about. Still, he gave no sign of wanting to pursue the matter.

"Captain . . ."

Picard whirled at the sound of Worf's voice. The Klingon was reacting to something he saw on his aft console.

"There are five Terellian transport ships holding position in the Devron system, sir."

"We're being hailed by the lead ship," added Tasha. "Their pilot's name is Androna."

"On screen," instructed the captain.

In the next instant, the viewscreen filled with the image of a Terellian. *"Enterprise,"* he said, smiling. "You are a welcome sight. We've been receiving threats from the Romulan Empire ever since we entered the Neutral Zone. I'm glad to see you're here to protect us."

Picard frowned. "Why have you come here?"

Androna's expression became even brighter. "Once we heard about the Light . . . about the power it has to heal illness, to rejuvenate the elderly . . . we *had* to come here."

The captain sighed. Judging by the looks on his officers' faces, they were rather confused. None of them, it seemed, had heard anything about this.

Of course, they hadn't just leaped through time. They hadn't been sitting there in Beverly Crusher's sickbay, where a man's eyes were growing younger, listening to reports of injuries that had healed themselves.

"We can't really be certain that the . . . Light . . . has this power," Picard replied. "And there may be dangers, side effects we're not aware of. . . ."

The Terellian wasn't moved. "I have five ships full of sick and dying people, Captain. If there's even a chance it's true, I can't turn back now."

However, the captain could be persistent too. "It would be safer for all concerned if you left the Neutral Zone . . . and let us investigate the phenomenon more fully."

Androna shook his head. "No, my friend. I've come too far. I choose to remain here."

Picard was frustrated with this response. Unfortunately, he didn't have the authority to order them away.

"I warn you," he said, "that if the Romulans should decide to intervene, I may not be able to protect you."

"I understand," answered the Terellian. "We'll take that risk. Good luck, Captain—to both of us."

A moment later, Androna's image was gone. Picard mulled the situation over for a moment, then headed for his ready room. As he passed Tasha, he said, "You have the bridge, Lieutenant."

She nodded. "Aye, sir."

The doors parted for him, giving him access to a place where he could stop and think for a moment. Where . . .

. . . nothing looked familiar. But then, why should it? He wasn't on the *Enterprise* any longer. He was in Beverly's ready room on the *Pasteur*.

Damn, thought Picard. I've shifted again.

As he moved toward the door, the deck suddenly bucked beneath his feet, nearly throwing him to the ground. Hearing the red-alert klaxon, he made use of whatever handholds presented themselves and ventured out uncertainly onto the bridge.

Beverly was sitting in the center seat, giving orders. But there was nothing on the viewscreen to explain why.

"What's going on?" he asked, loud enough to be heard.

Beverly turned in her seat. "We're under attack, Jean-Luc."

Just then, the ship was rocked again. But still, Picard couldn't pinpoint the cause of it.

"Shield strength down to fifty-two percent," called out Chilton. "Minor damage to the port nacelle."

Worf looked up from the console he'd commandeered. "Three Klingon attack cruisers have decloaked to port and starboard." His expression was not a joyous one. "We are surrounded!"

CHAPTER 19

A third time, the ship was walloped by Klingon fire. Holding tight to her armrests, Beverly gritted her teeth.

It had been a long time since she'd been in a battle—and she wasn't about to engage in one now, if she could help it. Especially not with the deck stacked so thoroughly against her.

She looked to Chilton and kept her tone as even as possible. "Warp speed, Ensign. Get us out of here!"

Chilton worked at her conn board. "I can't comply. Warp power off-line, sir."

Another jolt. This time, Beverly was nearly torn from her chair.

"Bring us about," she commanded. "Course one-four-eight mark two-one-five. Full impulse."

The ship came about, but it didn't do them much good. The Klingon attack cruisers were right on their tail. Yet again, they were raked by enemy fire. On the bridge, they felt the impact as a series of vicious jerks.

"Warp power fluctuating," Chilton announced. "Shields down to thirty percent."

Beverly bit her lip. Behind her, she heard a familiar voice make itself heard over the melee.

"Weapons status, Mr. Worf?"

For that one moment, Picard almost looked and sounded like his old self. It was as if he'd temporarily shrugged off the debilitating effects of his disease and become the master strategist again.

What's more, the answer he'd demanded wasn't long in coming. "These phasers are no match for their shields, sir. Our only hope is to escape."

Consumed with anger, Beverly whirled. "I thought you said I had eight hours, Worf. What the hell are they doing here now?"

"These must be ships from some other sector," the Klingon shot back. He frowned at his monitor, no doubt wondering why he hadn't foreseen this possibility.

Beverly turned to Geordi. "We need warp power—*now.*"

The former chief engineer worked at his console—but it didn't look good. Finally he raised his head.

"Sorry, Captain. They're just too much for us. I can't keep the phase inducers on-line any—"

He was interrupted by another bone-rattling blow to the ship.

"Shields down to nine percent," reported Chilton. "One more hit and they'll collapse entirely."

Beverly cursed under her breath. There was only one option left to her—and though she didn't like it, she'd have to exercise it.

"Worf," she said, "open a channel. Signal our surrender."

Thirty years ago, the Klingon would have protested, desperate to avoid even the appearance of cowardice. Older and wiser now, he simply complied.

They waited. A moment later, he looked up. But he didn't seem happy with the results.

"They will not accept our surrender," he informed them. "They intend to complete what they began."

Before she could assimilate the information, the ship lurched again under the Klingons' barrage, throwing her clear of the captain's chair. Before she hit the deck, she saw Chilton's console explode in a geyser of sparks, catching the ensign full in the face.

Jean-Luc, who was nearer to Chilton than anyone else, came to the woman's aid as quickly as he could. But Beverly could see that it was too late. Her ensign was dead.

Jean-Luc looked up and met Beverly's gaze. His expression reminded her that he'd lost people in much the same way.

In the meantime, Worf had taken over Chilton's duties from his aft console. "Our shields have collapsed," he remarked soberly. "We are defenseless against them."

Returning to her captain's chair, Beverly ignored her bruises and fixed her attention on the viewscreen. It showed only one of their pursuers, who had now taken up positions surrounding them.

She sighed raggedly. It was only a matter of time now. Seeing that their prey had nothing left, the Klingons would apply the death stroke. And, knowing them, they would be quick about it.

"Captain," said Data, "there's another ship de-cloaking—bearing two-one-five mark three-one-oh." Beverly turned to look at him, wondering why their adversaries needed reinforcements against a medical vessel.

The android looked surprised. "Captain . . . it's the *Enterprise!*"

Beverly's heart leapt at the mere mention of their old ship. Returning her attention to the viewscreen, she watched as the Galaxy-class vessel decloaked behind and above the unsuspecting Klingon cruiser.

Suddenly, the *Enterprise* let loose with a furious volley of phasers and photon torpedoes. Hammered beyond its capacity to defend itself, the attack cruiser shot apart in a cloud of blue plasma.

Before anyone on the *Pasteur* could celebrate, the medical ship pitched again. "Direct hit to the warp core," shouted Geordi. "Heavy damage . . ."

Jean-Luc's face went white with dread. "The warp core . . . we can't let that happen! We have to stabilize it!" he cried—and moved to help Geordi at the console.

"The Klingon ships are disengaging," Data declared.

However, the *Pasteur* was rocked yet again.

"But not without a few parting shots," the android added.

"Captain," Geordi bellowed, "I can't stabilize the core. It's going critical!"

Abruptly, a voice came through over their intercom grid—a voice that Beverly had heard before. *"Enterprise to Pasteur.* Our sensors show your ship has a warp-core breach in progress."

"Damned right it does!" she responded.

"Prepare for emergency beam-out," the voice advised.

Jean-Luc looked up in wonder. Then he turned to her, his eyes posing the question even before he could say the word.

"Riker?" he breathed.

"Riker," Beverly repeated, confirming it for him.

Jean-Luc seemed perplexed—and no wonder. Just a little while ago, his former exec had refused to help him. And now . . .

Before she could take her speculation any further, Beverly found herself standing on the bridge of the *Enterprise.* Will Riker was sitting in the center seat, as he had in the past when Jean-Luc was absent or off-duty. Except now, he looked a bit more comfortable there.

Of course, that came as no surprise. Will had commanded the *Enterprise* for several years after Jean-Luc joined the diplomatic corps—and before Riker himself became an admiral.

Beverly didn't recognize his crew, but she hadn't expected to. Hell, she hadn't expected *anything* except to be blasted to atoms.

Looking behind her, she saw that Jean-Luc, Worf, Data, Geordi, and her bridge officers—with the exception of poor Chilton—had materialized on the bridge as well. But what about the rest of her people?

She was answered by the officer at tactical. "The *Pasteur* crew is safely aboard, Admiral."

"Raise shields," responded Riker. "Where are the Klingons?"

The tactical officer consulted his board. "They're still moving off, sir—half a light-year distant."

The admiral nodded. "They'll be back," he said confidently.

But for now, Beverly assured herself, they were safe. Breathing a sigh of relief, she looked around appraisingly.

Apparently, the *Enterprise* had seen a few technological updates over the years. The captain's chair was slightly higher than it used to be, and there were other changes in evidence. But it was still basically the same place she had once called home.

Satisfied that the battle was over, Riker turned to the new arrivals and favored them with a smile. "Well?" he asked, only half-seriously. "Isn't somebody going to say thank you?"

Worf took a step toward the admiral. His face was racked with barely restrained fury.

"There is nothing to thank you *for*," he snarled, his mouth twisting around the words. "If you had not turned the captain down when he came to you for help, none of this would have happened."

Riker's smile disappeared. "What about you, Worf? I can't believe you let a defenseless ship cross into hostile territory without an escort."

"I did what was right," the Klingon insisted. His lips pulled back from his teeth. "Unlike some people," he grated, *"I* still have a sense of loyalty. Of honor."

"It wasn't a *question* of honor," said the admiral. "It was a question of common sense."

"Or of cowardice," spat Worf.

Riker's eyes flashed. "Remember who you're talking to, Governor."

Jean-Luc stepped between them before the confrontation could escalate any further. "We don't have time for this," he insisted. "Will, you have to shut down the warp-core breach on the *Pasteur*."

The admiral looked at him. "What?"

The older man nodded vigorously. "The subspace barrier in this region . . . it's very thin. If that ship explodes, it could rupture the barrier . . . flood this whole area with *anti-time!* Don't you see—this could be the very thing that destroys humanity!"

Oh, no, thought Beverly. Not that again.

Riker looked at Jean-Luc as if he had gone completely mad. Then he turned to Data, to Geordi, and, finally, to Beverly.

"What the hell's he talking about?"

She shook her head. "Frankly, I'm not sure anymore."

Jean-Luc grew wild. He grasped the android by the arm.

"Data, tell them! Tell them!"

The android met Riker's gaze. "The subspace barrier in this area is quite thin . . . though not unusually so."

"You see, you see?" Jean-Luc pointed to the viewscreen, where the *Pasteur* hung crippled in space, its hull charred by disruptor fire. "If that ship explodes, it could destroy everything!"

The admiral shot a glance at his tactical officer. "Mr. Gaines, is there any way to repair the warp-core breach on the *Pasteur?*"

The man didn't look optimistic. "I don't think so, sir. The plasma injector is already . . ."

Abruptly, something caught his eye. His fingers flew over his controls.

"Wait a minute, sir. I think it's about to breach. . . ."

Beverly focused on the viewscreen. For a moment, there was no change in the *Pasteur*'s status. Then, with shocking finality, the ship vanished in a burst of blue-white energy.

She felt a pang in her throat. The *Pasteur* was her first vessel . . . her first command. It was as if she had just seen a part of herself destroyed.

But Jean-Luc . . . his horror was much worse than hers, she observed. For, by his lights, the destruction of the *Pasteur* might well mean the end of all humanity.

CHAPTER 20

Picard stared at the screen in horror. Was this it? Was this the doom Q had foretold—the one he had failed to avoid, despite his advance knowledge of it?

Riker turned to his tactical officer. "Full scan, Mr. Gaines. Any sign of a subspace rupture?"

The man worked for a moment. Picard dreaded what he would hear.

But when Gaines looked up, he was hardly perturbed. "No, sir," he reported. "The subspace barrier is intact."

Everyone seemed to relax. Everyone, that is, except Picard himself. He didn't understand it, and he said so.

But Riker didn't seem to feel compelled to give him an explanation. "All right," said the big man. "Let's get out of here. Engage cloak."

"Cloak is not functioning," Gaines informed him. "We took a direct hit to the starboard plasma coil. Engineering reports seven hours until we can cloak again."

Riker frowned. "Then we'll do this the old-fashioned way. Lay in a course back to the Federation. Warp 13."

Picard shook his head. "No. We can't leave!"

The admiral gazed at him sympathetically. "We have to," he explained. "This is Klingon territory. We're not supposed to be here."

Picard felt himself growing desperate. Couldn't they see? This was more important than a silly political boundary. This was about *extinction*.

"No," he insisted, taking hold of Riker's tunic. "We have to stay here . . . to find the cause of the temporal anomaly. I caused it, dammit . . . though I don't know how . . ."

"Captain," the admiral said, pulling Picard's hand away from him, "there could be other attack cruisers on the way. We're getting out of here while we still can."

Picard was becoming frantic. He knew how hysterical he sounded, but he had to get through to them—to show them how important it was.

"We can't! We can't! Will, please . . . everything depends on this! Please listen to me!"

Too late, he caught sight of the hypospray in Beverly's hand. He started to turn, to fend it off, but he was too slow. He heard a hiss as the doctor released the spray's contents into his bloodstream.

Fighting the instantaneous effects, he lurched forward . . .

. . . and nearly bumped into a crewman as he came around a bend in the corridor.

The man, an engineering officer, apologized as he stepped to the side. "Sorry, sir."

"That's quite all right," Picard assured him. Judging by the man's uniform—and his own—he was back in the present. Without another word, he proceeded along the corridor.

But where was he going? Slowing down, he thought for a moment.

Sickbay. Of course. Beverly had asked him to come down there. She'd said that she wanted to speak with him.

Speeding up his pace, he negotiated another bend and saw the sickbay doors up ahead on his right. Narrowing the gap, he wondered what the doctor wanted to see him about.

Was it Geordi? Had something changed with regard to his condition?

The doors parted as he came near. Making his way through them, he saw that Beverly wasn't at the engineer's bed at all.

She was at another one—tending to Alissa Ogawa. The nurse was lying down, wearing a patient's gown. And—unless the captain's eyes were going bad—she no longer appeared to be pregnant.

Picard watched as Ogawa's husband went to her side. He took her hand, tried to comfort her—but the nurse was too distraught. She didn't want to be comforted.

Obviously, there was something wrong here. Something *very* wrong.

Slowly, not wishing to be any more obtrusive than necessary in the face of Ogawa's suffering, the captain moved to Beverly's side. She noticed him standing there right away.

He asked, "You wanted to see me, Doctor?"

"Yes," she replied. And then, to Ogawa: "I'll be right back, Alissa."

The nurse acknowledged her with a nod. Satisfied that Ogawa would be all right for the moment, Beverly took the captain aside and spoke to him in hushed tones.

"What is it?" he breathed. "What's wrong?"

"Alissa lost the baby," she told him, a shiver in her voice showing how much she shared in her assistant's sorrow.

Picard scowled. "What happened?" he asked.

The doctor looked at him. "I think it's the same thing that happened to Geordi. Somehow, the temporal energy from the anomaly caused the fetal tissue to revert to an earlier stage of development. It was as if the unborn child began to grow *younger* . . . and younger still . . . until finally, the DNA itself began to break down."

The captain tilted his head to indicate the nurse. "How is she?"

Beverly shrugged. "Physically, she's fine—at least, for now. But if this temporal reversion continues, I don't think any of us are going to be fine for much longer." A pause. "I scanned most of the crew. The temporal energy is beginning to affect everyone, Jean-Luc."

He didn't like the direction in which this conversation was headed. "How?" he inquired.

The doctor sighed. "Our cellular structures are changing. Instead of dividing, our cells are coming together . . . reverting to earlier cellular structures. In some cases, this has caused old injuries to be healed . . . but that's only the tip of the iceberg. Eventually, this could kill us all, as it did Nurse Ogawa's baby."

It was a horrible prospect. Picard's lips pressed together as he contemplated it.

"How widespread is the effect?" he wondered. "Is it localized to this area, or could it affect other areas of space?"

Beverly shook her head. "I don't know."

The captain couldn't take any chances. "Send a report to Starbase Twenty-Three," he said. "They're the nearest outpost. Have them begin checking their personnel for these effects."

"Will do," she assured him. As he watched, she moved across sickbay to put the order into effect.

Picard took another look at Ogawa. Could *this* be the catastrophe Q had warned him of? Was humanity going to devolve into the single-celled creatures that had been its primeval forebears?

He set his teeth. Not if *he* could help it.

Looking up, he said, "Mr. Data."

The android's reply over the intercom system was crisp and immediate. "Aye, sir?"

"Meet me in the observation lounge," the captain told him.

"On my way," said Data.

A few minutes later, Picard found himself studying a padd in the ship's observation lounge as Data looked on. It contained an outline of the android's initial findings regarding the spatial anomaly.

Finished, the captain looked up and eyed Data across

the polished expanse of the lounge's table. "Fascinating," he commented.

"Indeed," said the android.

"And how long until we've *completed* the tachyon scan?" Picard inquired.

Data hardly found it necessary to think about it. "Approximately one hour, forty-five minutes, sir."

The captain nodded. "Good. Once that's done, I want you to analyze the information and find a way to shut the anomaly down. But I don't want to do anything that will exacerbate the problem."

"I could prepare a risk analysis on whatever solution I devise," the android suggested.

"Good idea," Picard confirmed.

"Thank you, sir," replied Data. And without any further ado, he made his exit, intent on the task ahead of him.

The captain watched him go, then picked up the padd and walked over to the observation portal. He was just starting to feel that they might have a fighting chance against the anomaly . . .

. . . when someone cried out in a strident voice, "Seven! A winner!"

Turning, the captain was shocked to see that the observation-lounge table was gone. In its place was an old-fashioned craps table, straight out of some archaic Earth casino—a table covered with green felt and host to several small piles of plastic chips.

A pair of dice sat on the end closest to Picard. One showed a set of three dots, the other a set of four. The total? *Seven.*

Looking up, he saw that Q was standing at the opposite end of the table, dressed as a twentieth-century croupier. Tossing some chips to the human, the entity used his croupier's stick to rake in the dice.

"Place your bets," he called out, "place your bets. New shooter, new shooter comin' up."

The captain glared at him. "What do you want this time, Q?"

Q shrugged. "I'm just here as an observer, Jean-Luc. I want to see what kind of bet you're going to make on this anomaly."

Picard stiffened. What was this about? "I'm not betting anything," he declared.

"Oh, yes you are," Q argued. "And the stakes on this table are pretty high. The highest, in fact."

With his stick, he indicated a small sign on the table. It read: TABLE MINIMUM—HUMANITY OR THE RACE OF YOUR CHOICE. The captain was not amused in the least.

"You sure you want Data to shut down that temporal anomaly?" Q pressed. He picked up the dice and rolled them around in his hand.

Picard looked at him. "Are you suggesting that by shutting the anomaly down, I will cause the destruction of mankind?"

Q shook his head. "I'm not suggesting anything, my friend. I just run the table." Picking up some chips, he began to place a bet. "Let's see . . . you've bet on the temporal anomaly at four to one. Shall we see what comes up?"

As Q threw the dice . . .

* * *

. . . the captain found himself on a craggy ledge.

Looking down, he saw that he was perched high above a vast, chaotic soup—a miasma of steaming lava and bubbling gases. It was hot here, so oppressively hot that he already found himself perspiring, and the air was full of fine, black flecks.

"Welcome home," said Q, who was standing beside him, still dressed in his croupier's outfit.

"Home?" echoed Picard, wiping the sweat from his forehead. He honestly didn't know what his companion was talking about.

"Don't you recognize your old stomping grounds?" asked Q. "This is Earth—France, in fact. About . . . oh . . . three and a half billion years ago, give or take an eon or so." He wrinkled his nose. "Smells awful, doesn't it . . . all that sulfur and volcanic ash . . . I really must speak to the maid."

The captain turned to him, his eyes stinging from the debris in the atmosphere. "Is there a point to all this, or are we just on another of your merry travelogues?"

The entity looked at him. "Travelogues? You wound me, Jean-Luc. All I'm doing is trying to further your miserable education."

"Indeed," Picard commented. "And exactly what am I to learn in this place? How to asphyxiate myself?"

Q smiled knowingly and pointed to the sky. "Look!" he exclaimed. "Pretty impressive, wouldn't you say?"

As Picard followed the gesture, his mouth went even drier. All he could see, from horizon to horizon, filling the heavens with its ominous brilliance, was the spatial anomaly that they'd located in the Devron system.

But here, it was even *bigger*.

"The anomaly is here?" wondered the captain. "At Earth . . . ?"

"At this point in history," Q explained, "the anomaly is everywhere. It has filled this entire quadrant of your galaxy."

Picard's eyes were watering from the ashes in the air. He dabbed at them, to no avail.

"The further back in time I go . . . the larger the anomaly." He tried to make sense of that. "But—"

Abruptly, Q took off along the length of the ledge, as if he'd caught a glimpse of something he couldn't resist. "Jean-Luc, quickly—there's something over here I want you to see!"

Beckoning enthusiastically, Q knelt by a small muddy pond at one end of their ledge. The captain went over to see what Q was looking at.

Together, they peered down into the water. It was murky, almost impenetrable to the naked eye . . . but free of the algae one might normally see in such a place.

"What am I looking at?" asked Picard finally.

"Looking at?" repeated Q. "Why, *mon capitaine,* this is *you.* And may I say you've never looked better."

The captain found himself becoming annoyed. Q was toying with him. He *hated* that, with a passion.

"Me, Q?"

"I'm serious, Jean-Luc. Well, in a manner of speaking. You see," he said, pointing, "right here, life is about to form on this planet for the very first time. Two proteins are about to combine and form the first amino acid— one of the building blocks of what you laughingly call *life.*"

Despite himself, Picard was intrigued. Impossible as it

was to see anything, he couldn't help but lean closer to the surface of the pond.

Q turned to him and spoke in his most mysterious, conspiratorial whisper. "Strange, isn't it? Everything you know . . . your entire civilization . . . it all begins right here in this little pond of goo. Disgustingly appropriate somehow, isn't it?" He grunted. "Too bad you didn't bring a microscope. This is quite fascinating, don't you think?"

Pointing into the depths of the pond—at something no human could hope to discern, of course—Q provided a blow-by-blow description of the action. "Here they go . . . the two proteins are moving closer . . . closer . . . *closer* . . ."

Suddenly, he recoiled, disappointment etched into his features. "Oh, no! Why . . . nothing happened! Nothing at all!"

Picard stared at him through eyes rubbed raw by primordial pollution. "What do you mean, nothing happened? Don't tell me you stopped it!"

Q looked at him and wagged his finger. "Now, Jean-Luc, we've talked at length about your incessant need to blame me for all your problems. *You* did this all by your lonesome, I assure you."

The captain frowned. "I did nothing, Q."

Q stood. *"Au contraire."* He pointed to the sky. "You did *that*. And *that* disrupted the beginning of life."

Removing the pair of dice from his pocket, he showed them to Picard. "You see? *Snake eyes.* You lose."

The captain glanced at the dice. They had turned up snake eyes, all right. But the dice weren't the ultimate arbiter of his fate; they couldn't be.

Despite the omens Q had presented to him, there was still a chance that he would find a way out of this . . . a way to preserve humanity. He looked up, intending to question Q further . . .

. . . and realized he was looking at Deanna Troi instead. By her uniform and her hairstyle, he could tell that he was back in the past.

It was funny how well he was adjusting to his transits through time. The feelings of disorientation were now at a minimum.

Looking around, he saw that he was on the bridge. O'Brien, Data, Tasha, and Worf were at their usual stations.

Troi spoke as if she were answering a question he had just posed to her. "Dr. Selar has reported that twenty-three children on board have contracted some kind of illness. She said their tissues appear to be . . . reverting to some earlier state of development."

Oh, no, he thought. Not here, too.

She paused, well aware that he wouldn't like what she had to tell him—not knowing he appreciated the nature of the problem better than she did. "She thinks it's being caused by the anomaly, sir."

Picard nodded, then turned to Tasha. "Lieutenant, inform Starfleet Command that we believe the anomaly has toxic effects."

"I already have," she said. A beat. "They've ordered us to withdraw from the Neutral Zone and to escort the pilgrim ships back to Federation territory."

The captain considered the order grimly. "Tell

Starfleet we're remaining here," he replied. "However, we'll tell the pilgrim ships to withdraw." He turned to the android. "Mr. Data, as soon as the tachyon scan is complete, I want you to—"

Tasha interrupted. "I'm afraid I can't let you do that, sir."

Picard was surprised. He faced her. "What?"

The security chief straightened, her resolve evident in her every feature. "We've received direct orders to leave the Neutral Zone, sir. There are children dying—children we may be able to save if we act now. And our presence here is in direct violation of the Treaty of Algeron."

The captain remained calm, despite the stakes they were playing for. "Are you questioning my orders, Lieutenant?"

Tasha took a breath. "Yes, sir . . . I am. And unless you take this ship back to Federation territory . . . I'm prepared to relieve you and take command of this vessel."

Picard hadn't been prepared for that. He looked around and saw that the rest of the bridge crew was watching the confrontation.

Obviously, he told himself, this was going to be a lot more difficult than he'd anticipated.

CHAPTER **21**

Picard eyed Tasha. He wanted to tell her that they would grow to know and trust each other. He wanted to say that, one day, she would be willing to lay down her life for him.

But he couldn't. He had to tread a thin line here, and apprising his officers of what was in store for them was outside that line.

For now, all he could do was appeal to his officers' pride and integrity . . . their sense of justice and discipline. And then hope that that would be enough.

"Lieutenant, you are coming close to mutiny," he warned her. "Dangerously close."

Worf stepped forward. He was younger and more hotheaded than the Worf the captain was now used to.

"It would not be mutiny," the Klingon reminded them, "if the ship's counselor certified you unfit to command."

All eyes fell on Troi. But she didn't react—at least, not yet.

Abruptly, O'Brien stood. "Here, now," he said. "There's no cause for all this. It's not our place to question the captain's orders."

Obviously, Tasha felt otherwise. She looked at the counselor. "Deanna?"

Troi frowned as she felt the burden of her task. It was all up to her now.

She looked at Picard—seeking information not only with her eyes, but with her Betazoid talents. "Captain," she asked, *"do* you intend to obey the order from Starfleet?"

There were a number of ways he could have handled the situation, a number of ways he could have answered her. But the counselor would detect any attempt at subterfuge.

In the end, he opted for the simple truth. "No," he replied. "I do not."

There were gasps and murmurs all around the bridge. Apparently, his officers hadn't expected to hear him say that.

"I'm sure," he went on, "that makes me sound quite irrational to you all."

"Irrational may not be the correct word," observed Data. "Your course of action so far does not imply a lack of reason, but a lack of explanation. You seem to have a hidden agenda that you are unwilling to share with the rest of us." A beat. "If I were to describe you, I would say you are being . . . surreptitious, secretive, reticent, clandestine—"

Picard cut him off. "Thank you, Commander. I get the point."

Nonetheless, he knew that the android had spoken for his crewmates. From their point of view, he *was* being secretive and surreptitious. It was time to clear the air.

As the captain spoke, he moved around the bridge, addressing every member of the crew with a glance. After all, if he was going to get them on his side, he had to make them feel like he was one of them.

"So," he said, "you all want an explanation . . . and I could give you one. I could tell you that an omnipotent being from another space-time continuum has been shifting me through three time periods . . . that he has threatened the destruction of mankind . . . and that it is up to me to save humanity. But you would probably call me insane."

"Insane may not be the appropriate term . . ." Data began.

Troi stilled him with a sharp look. "Please," she told him. "Not now."

The android stopped, unoffended. How naive he had been during those earliest days, Picard reflected. How artless.

"However," he continued, "since I can't give you a logical, rational explanation for what I'm doing . . ." He turned to Troi. "It all falls on your shoulders, Deanna. Have I really demonstrated a lack of mental competence . . . or evil intent? Or am I simply following my own conscience . . . trying to do what I believe is best for the ship, and for the Federation?"

He waited while she probed and reprobed his consciousness, scanning for signs of malice or duplicity. She wouldn't find any, of course.

Still, there were things he was holding back. The counselor would discover that, if she hadn't already. And having discovered it, she might interpret it as a reason not to trust him.

A moment later, she announced her verdict. "You're right," she told the captain. "I don't sense any mental instability or malicious intent. Therefore, I can see no grounds to find you unfit for command." She paused. "But I am extremely worried about the actions you are taking . . . and I would strongly urge you to reconsider."

Picard nodded. "Your concerns are noted." Then, turning to Tasha, he said, "You can still attempt to relieve me, if you wish."

The security chief shook her head. "No, sir," she responded. "I may be many things, but I'm not a mutineer. If Troi says you're fit for command, then I'll do my duty."

It was clear that she still had misgivings about him. However, for Tasha, her duty to her captain came first. Picard was grateful for that.

"Very well, then, Lieutenant. Contact the lead Terellian ship. Tell them we'll be evacuating all civilians and nonessential personnel from the *Enterprise* to their vessels. Once we've completed the evacuation, they are to leave the Neutral Zone."

The security officer was already at work, even before the captain could complete his instructions. "Aye, sir," she answered.

"And, Lieutenant . . ." he continued.

She looked up at him.

"Don't take no for an answer," he told her.

Tasha nodded. "I won't, sir."

Turning to his conn and ops officers, Picard said, "Data . . . O'Brien . . . you're with me." As they followed his order, other personnel took their places.

Waiting just a moment for them to fall in behind him, he led the way to the turbolift.

Several minutes later, down in engineering, Picard was peering at Data and O'Brien across the master systems display console.

The android seemed just the slightest bit frustrated. "Captain, I do not see any way to dissipate the anomaly," he said.

O'Brien swore softly. Being human, his emotions ran a good deal higher.

"Sir," he said, "the anomaly's output is greater than the combined energy of our entire fleet. It's just too big for us to handle."

Picard thought for a moment. "Let's concentrate on how this anomaly was initially formed. Speculation?"

Data was the first to respond. "Temporal ruptures in the space-time continuum are rarely a naturally occurring phenomenon. It is therefore most likely that this anomaly was caused by an outside catalyst."

"Like a warp-core explosion," O'Brien suggested.

"I think I can rule out a warp-core explosion," said the captain.

The android thought some more. "Our tachyon pulse

has been unable to completely penetrate the anomaly. If we had information about the center of the phenomenon, we might have a basis for speculation."

"Can you find a way to scan the interior?"

"I've tried everything I know of," O'Brien said quickly. "There's just too much interference. There's nothing on board that'll do the job."

Picard thought quickly. "Do you know what would?"

There was a tense moment, then Data answered. "In theory, a tomographic imaging scanner capable of multiphasic resolution would be able to penetrate this much interference." He paused. "Sir, the Daystrom Institute has been working on such a device, although it is still only theoretical."

Information, Picard thought, we need to know what's going on inside that thing. The question is—

—how to *get* that information. Abruptly, he realized that he'd shifted again. He was no longer in the past, in engineering. Now he was back in the present, at the aft science station on the *Enterprise*'s bridge.

Data was still with him. But instead of O'Brien, he now had Geordi.

More important, there was an opportunity here, if he could only seize it. In the past, they'd determined a way to get more information about the anomaly's internal workings—but they'd lacked the technology to do so.

"Mr. Data," he said. "Do we have a tomographic imaging scanner on board?"

"Yes, sir," the android replied.

"Can you use it to scan the center of the anomaly?"

The android turned to him. "Possibly." He moved to do so. "Sir, there is a great deal of interference . . . but I am getting some readings." Picard waited impatiently while Data pushed buttons on his console. "This is very unusual," Data said, with just a hint of the inflection Picard remembered from Data's future self.

"What is it?" Picard asked. At last he felt they were closing in on the core of the problem.

"It appears that our tachyon pulse is converging with two other tachyon pulses at the center of the anomaly. The other two pulses have the exact same amplitude modulation as our own pulse. It is as if all three originated from the *Enterprise.*"

Picard considered that. "Three pulses . . . from three time periods . . . all converging at one point in space. . . ." It had to be more than a coincidence.

"Captain," Data asked, "what are you suggesting?"

Picard massaged his jaw. "Just that . . ."

". . . that . . ."

Damn. He'd shifted again, hadn't he? Picard was lying on a bed in some sort of guest quarters. He was wearing a set of loose-fitting blue nightclothes. And he was old again, so this had to be the future.

How had he gotten here? He scratched at his bearded chin. The last thing he remembered in this era was . . .

Oh, yes. Back on the bridge. Beverly had used a hypospray on him. And he was only now waking up.

Sitting up, he swiveled his legs over and got out of bed.

Noting a familiar-looking control on a nearby table, he tapped it.

"Computer," he said, "where's Admiral Riker?"

"Admiral Riker is in Ten-Forward," came the response.

Picard harrumphed and headed for the door. In the other two time periods, he was moving toward a solution to the problem posed by the anomaly. He was determined that, no matter what it took, this time period would be no different.

CHAPTER **22**

Admiral Will Riker glanced over his shoulder at a table on the other end of Ten-Forward, where Geordi and Worf were sitting together. Then, he looked back to Beverly and Data, with whom he was sharing *this* table.

He had tried to make his glance as casual as possible. Unfortunately, Beverly knew him too well to believe it.

"Spying on the enemy?" she asked sarcastically.

Riker grunted. "In a manner of speaking."

"Will," said the doctor, "how long is this thing between you and Worf going to go on?"

He shrugged. "It's been going on for twenty years now. And it doesn't look like it's going to end any time soon."

"I suspect the last thing Counselor Troi would have wanted is for the two of you to be alienated from one another," Data remarked.

"I agree," Dr. Crusher put in. "It's time to put this behind you."

"I tried, at Deanna's funeral," Riker replied sadly. He recalled that tragic day. "He wouldn't talk to me."

"Might have been tough for him then," Geordi suggested. "He took her death pretty hard."

"Yeah?" Riker said, his voice sharper than he would have liked. "Well, he wasn't the only one." He saw Dr. Crusher's deep-set eyes lock straight onto his.

"I know," the doctor said, "but in his mind . . . you were the reason he and Deanna never got together."

"I didn't do anything to stand in their way," Riker answered, his natural defensiveness coming forward.

The doctor's bright eyes still held him. "Didn't you, Will?" she asked softly.

"Did I?" he answered, as if asking himself a question. "I just . . . never could admit it was over. I kept thinking one day we'd get together again . . . and then she was gone." Riker stopped, took a deep, sad, breath. "You think you've got all the time in the world, until . . ." His voice and his thoughts drifted off.

He recalled the last time he had seen Worf. It was on Betazed, at a place called Lake Cataria . . . where the sky was such a deep violet-blue it hurt one's eyes to look at it, and the breeze from the mountains carried the scent of something strangely like chocolate.

It was a perfect day—the kind that made one wish there would never be an end to it. The breeze was warm there, but not too warm. And the water of the lake sparkled like liquid gold in the burnished sunshine.

They had all gathered by the sandy western shore— Riker and the Klingon, the captain and Beverly, Geordi and Data. It was where they would say their farewells to

the woman who had been their friend and confidante
. . . their comrade and advisor.

Lwaxana, on whom age and sorrow and loss were at
last taking their toll, had made her apologies through her
giant of a servant. She would not come to the public
ceremony. Unable to bear the sorrow of seeing them all
again, she would do her mourning in private.

Betazoid custom called for a wooden funeral platform, on which the deceased could be viewed in a
transparent case. In this instance, the platform was
empty, since there was nothing left of the deceased to
inter.

A friend of the family led them in the traditional
funeral chants, much of which was snatched away by the
wind. And when the time came to speak of her, he did so
out loud, because they were offworlders and not
telepaths.

Mostly, he spoke of Deanna's courage—and how,
though the bounty of her heart brought great joy to those
around her, it also made her vulnerable to those whose
hearts were full of bitterness. In the end, he said, that
vulnerability was her undoing.

Then he called upon the one who had been closest to
her to plant the first seeds in the soil before the platform.
Riker and Worf glared at each other across the patch
of freshly turned earth. Riker saw in Worf's eyes the
pain that was a reflection of his own. Then he
gave way, letting Worf have the honor of planting the
seeds.

He hoped that somehow this would help make things
right between him and Worf, but he doubted it. Klingons
were good at holding grudges.

With a start, he remembered he was in Ten-Forward.

"You can't go back," the doctor was saying. "But maybe you can still salvage the present."

Focusing his eyes, Riker looked at her. "Sure," he said. "And maybe latinum will start growing on trees."

She leaned forward, undaunted. "Talk to him, Will. Let him know you regret what happened." A wistful smile crossed her face. "Deanna would've wanted it that way."

He knew in his heart that she was right. That *was* the way Deanna would've wanted it. But that didn't mean it was something he could do.

Dammit, thought Picard. Dammit to hell. When had they reconfigured all the corridors on this ship?

Of course, he knew that they hadn't done any such thing. But it certainly *seemed* as if they had. Though he had once known these streamlined hallways like those in his family's house, he now felt utterly lost.

Pausing at an intersection, he looked first one way and then the other. Which way to go? He wasn't at all sure. And the fact that he was drawing curious looks from passing crew members didn't make it any easier to figure things out.

Finally, Picard chose a direction and proceeded down the corridor. After a moment or two, it looked promising. And then, at long last, he saw the set of doors that he'd been looking for.

As he approached triumphantly, they opened and he prepared to confront Riker . . . but found himself staring into one of the transporter rooms instead of Ten-

Forward. Swearing beneath his breath, he turned away and resumed his ever more frustrating search.

Continuing down the corridor, he decided that this time he was going in the right direction. But when he came to another intersection, he found himself flustered again. It was no use. Everything looked too much like everything else. How ridiculous, he thought . . . he couldn't find his way in a ship he had once commanded.

Finally, he stopped a passing ensign. "How do I . . . how do I get to Ten-Forward?" he asked.

The young man couldn't help but stare at Picard's garb. Still, he was helpful enough to point at the ceiling. "Two decks up, sir. You want section zero-zero-five."

"Thank you," the captain told him. Pulling his night-clothes more closely about him, as if trying to gather up the last, remaining shreds of his dignity, he headed back in the direction of the nearest turbolift.

Sitting there in Ten-Forward, considering the rueful expression on Admiral Riker's face, Data couldn't help but reflect that there were areas of human nature he might never fully understand.

"Oh, my god," said Beverly.

It was her tone of voice, as much as the actual words, that caused Data to turn and follow her gesture. When he had done so, he clearly saw the reason for her exclamation.

Captain Picard had entered Ten-Forward in his night-clothes. It was a remarkably inappropriate act; even Data could see that. By comparison, the gray streak in his hair was a thing of great subtlety.

The captain moved directly to the table occupied by

Worf and Admiral Riker. His eyes were wide with excitement.

"Will!" he cried. "I know what's happening . . . I know what causes the anomaly. We have to go back!"

The admiral just stared at him, openmouthed. Before he knew it, Data found himself approaching the table. Geordi and Dr. Crusher were not far behind him, motivated by concern for their former leader.

By the time they got there, Riker was shaking his head in disbelief. "Listen, Jean-Luc. The only place you're going is back to bed."

The captain was frantic. He shook his fists at the air.

"Dammit, Will, I *know* what's going on. *We're* causing the anomaly . . . with a . . . with the tachyon pulse. It happened in all three . . . in all three . . . *We did it in all three time periods!"*

Dr. Crusher placed her hand on Picard's shoulder. "Jean-Luc, you'd better come with me."

But the captain jerked away from her. "Leave me alone!" he croaked. "I'm not crazy."

Data had his doubts about that. It seemed that Picard was farther gone than he had thought.

"The tachyon pulses," the older man ranted. "They were used in the same spot. The same location in all three time periods . . . don't you see?"

The doctor tried again to calm him down. "Jean-Luc . . . please . . ."

But Picard persisted. "When the tachyon pulse used the . . . I mean, when the *Pasteur* used the tachyon pulse, *we* set the . . . you know, we . . . we started everything. We set it in motion."

The android felt badly for him. He knew what it was like to lose one's faculties. There had been several times during his stint on the *Enterprise* when he'd been partially or completely incapacitated.

However, those had been temporary conditions. He had never had to endure a slow and painful deterioration, as in the captain's case—or to face the certainty that, one day, he would lose his faculties entirely.

"It's like . . . the chicken and the egg!" rambled Picard. "You think it started back then . . . but it didn't. It started here, in the future. That's why . . . why it gets larger in the past . . ."

Larger in the past . . . ?

The android tilted his head slightly as he considered that. How *strange*. Though it seemed to be merely a component of a sick man's ravings, there was a certain logic to the statement as well.

Was it possible that the captain knew what he was talking about after all? Data thought for a moment—and only a moment. He was, after all, an artificial intelligence.

Admiral Riker hit his comm badge. "Riker to security. We have a problem in Ten-Forward. Send a team to—"

Data spoke up. "Just a moment, sir. I believe I understand what the captain is saying."

The admiral looked at him. "You do?"

"Yes. If I'm not mistaken, he is describing a *paradox.*"

Picard held his trembling fists out to the android. "Yes! Yes, exactly!"

Data began to pace. He had become accustomed to doing his best thinking that way. And besides, it seemed like a very professorial thing to do.

"Let us assume for the moment," he said, "that the

captain has indeed been traveling through time. Let us also assume he has initiated an inverse tachyon pulse at the same location in space in all three time periods."

"Go on," instructed Geordi. Obviously, he was intrigued, now that Data had gotten into the act.

"In that case," the android continued, "it is possible that the tachyon beams could've transited through the subspace barrier and caused an anti-time rupture. This rupture would manifest itself as a spatial anomaly."

"Right," said the former chief engineer. "I see where you're going. The anomaly is an eruption of anti-time . . . and because it operates in the opposite way *normal time* does, the effects would run *backward* through the space-time continuum."

"Yes!" rasped Picard. "That's why the anomaly was larger in the past . . . than in the future. It was growing as it traveled backward through time."

The doctor shook her head. "Wait a minute. We didn't see any evidence of an anti-time reaction in the Devron system."

"Not *yet!*" insisted the captain. "Chicken and the egg! You see?"

"Indeed," agreed Data.

It was remarkable how all Picard's seeming fantasies were coming together. He wished that he had seen the solution earlier.

"In a true paradox," he explained, "effect sometimes precedes cause. Therefore, the anomaly the captain saw in the past existed *before* we came to the Devron system and initiated the tachyon pulse."

They all looked at one another. "All right," said Riker.

"Let's say, for the moment, you're on the money. How do we prove any of this?"

"Go back," the captain advised. "Go back to the Devron system. It'll be there this time—I know it."

Data looked at the others. "He may be right. If our tachyon pulse contributed to a rupture in the fabric of anti-time, it may not have developed immediately. A return to the Devron system might show us the initial formation of the anomaly."

It was up to the admiral. Knowing that, everyone looked at him, waiting to see what he would do. After a long beat, he hit his comm badge.

"Riker to bridge. Set course for the Devron system. Maximum warp."

"Aye, sir," came the voice that Data now recognized as that of Lieutenant Gaines.

In the next moment, the admiral was on his feet, leading them to the exit. Everyone except Worf followed —causing Riker to stop and look back.

"Worf, we could use a hand," he said simply.

Worf considered for a moment, then followed.

CHAPTER 23

It felt good to be back in his clothes again, thought Picard. It was bad enough to *be* a little crazy. Looking the part only made matters that much worse.

As he stood on the bridge with Riker, Beverly, Data, Worf, and Geordi, he could almost imagine it was twenty-five years ago, and he was once again in his prime. Then, he had been the man on whom the fates of more than a thousand people depended. Now, he was lucky to have established some control over his own, meager existence.

"Entering the Devron system," announced the man at tactical. What was his name again?

"Thank you, Mr. Gaines," said Riker. "All stop."

That's right, Picard told himself. It was *Gaines*. He would do his best not to forget again—though he knew better than to make any promises in this time period.

Data, who had taken up a position next to La Forge at one of the aft consoles, looked up from his monitor.

"Sensors are picking up a small temporal anomaly off the port bow," he reported.

A . . . temporal anomaly? Then there *was* one in this time period. Picard felt that he was on the verge of being vindicated.

"On screen," ordered the admiral. His tone indicated that he wasn't quite ready to believe it.

But a moment later, the proof was handed to him on a latinum platter. Or, to be more accurate about it, on the viewscreen—where they could now make out a very small version of the anomaly.

Picard nodded. He had been right. But he didn't feel victorious—just vastly relieved.

"It's an anti-time eruption, all right," called Geordi, who'd scanned it. "It seems to have formed in the last six hours." He paused, calling for more information from the sensors. "And it's getting bigger."

"We can't let that happen," said Picard. "We've got to stop it here in the future . . . so it won't be able to travel back through time. . . ."

Riker looked at him. He knew better now than to believe the captain was just raving.

He turned to the android. "All right, Data. We need a solution and we need it fast."

The professor looked up from his monitor. As always, he seemed to have a response on the tip of his tongue.

"Since this anomaly has been formed by a convergence of tachyon pulses from three different time periods," he reasoned, "my first suggestion would be to shut down the pulses in the other two time periods."

A good idea, thought Picard. "The next time I'm there," he promised, "that's the first thing I'll do."

"But in case that doesn't work," the admiral added, "we're going to need a fallback solution."

Data nodded. "Understood, sir. I'm on it."

As the android went back to work, Beverly moved to Picard's side. "Jean-Luc," she said, "you look tired. Why don't you sit down?"

"Beverly," he rasped, "don't nursemaid me."

"It's not nursemaiding," she argued. "It's helping you to apply your resources more efficiently."

"Nursemaiding," Picard insisted volubly. Moving away from her . . .

. . . he saw that he was back at the aft consoles with Geordi and Data. Back in the *present.*

"Data," he snapped, seeing his opportunity. "Disengage the tachyon pulse. *Quickly.*"

The android looked up at him. "Sir?"

"Just do it," demanded the captain. "The convergence of tachyon pulses from the three time periods is what's causing the anomaly."

Data considered the implications at a speed even a computer might have envied. "Aye, sir," he responded, and got to work. "Tachyon pulse disengaged," he announced.

"Is there any change in the anomaly?" Picard asked . . .

. . . and found himself in his command chair, addressing the Data of the past—who was looking back over his shoulder from his position at ops. "No, sir," the android reported.

"Disengage the tachyon pulse," commanded the captain.

Data seemed about to ask a question, but refrained. Turning to his console, he performed the necessary manipulations.

After a moment, Picard asked, "Is it disengaged?"

The android swiveled again in his seat. "Aye, sir. However, it appears not to have had any measurable effect."

Picard frowned . . .

. . . and realized he was back in the future—though he was still sitting in the captain's chair. Immediately, he turned to his former comrades.

"I've shut off the tachyon pulses," he announced. "The ones in the other time periods."

This drew a few curious looks from the others, but no one called him crazy—or even suggested it. Apparently, they now accepted that he was traveling through time.

Picard fixed his gaze on Data. In the past, the android had informed him that their disengagement had had no effect—at least, none that was immediately apparent.

Perhaps in this time frame, it would be different. "What's happening with . . . with regard to the anomaly, Data?"

The android shook his head. "It is still growing larger," he reported with some reluctance.

"But Captain Picard has shut off the pulses," remarked Worf.

"True," said Data. "However, his actions do not seem to have created the desired effect."

Picard cursed inwardly. He had been so certain that it would work . . .

"What do we do?" asked Beverly.

La Forge let out a sigh of exasperation. "The only way to stop this thing is to repair the rupture at its focal point . . . where time and anti-time are converging."

"And how do we do that?" inquired Riker.

"It would require taking the ship *into* the anomaly," replied the android. His tone was matter-of-fact, as if he were lecturing one of his classes instead of facing a threat to the very fabric of reality. "Once inside," he went on, "we may be able to use our engines to create a static warp shell."

La Forge nodded. "Yes . . . and the shell would act like a *new* subspace barrier—separating time and anti-time."

"Exactly," said Data. "Collapsing the anomaly and . . . restoring the normal flow of time." He turned to Picard. "But this would have to be done in the other two time periods, as well."

The captain considered the prospect. "That could be a problem," he decided. "The anomaly's so much larger in the other two time periods . . ."

". . . it could be difficult to take the ship in."

He'd already finished his sentence before he looked up and saw that he was in the past again. Everyone on the bridge was looking at him.

"Take the ship in where, sir?" asked O'Brien.

Picard took a moment to make his decision. "Into the anomaly, Chief. Lay in a course to the exact center."

His officers were shocked.

"Captain," said Tasha, "you can't be serious. The energies in that thing could—"

The captain whirled. "I know that no one here understands this—but it is vital that we take the ship to the center of that phenomenon and create a static warp shell."

"A warp shell . . . ?" Troi repeated. She didn't look confident that such a thing could even be done.

"The endeavor you describe would place the ship at great risk," Data pointed out, perhaps unnecessarily.

"Yes," Picard admitted freely. "That's true. But you must believe I am doing this for a greater purpose."

He paused, wondering how to convey the importance of what he was asking of them. It wouldn't be easy.

"The stakes," he said, "are larger than any of you can imagine. The very existence of humanity depends on what we do here today."

The captain scanned their faces, one after the other. He had yet to sway them; he could see that. They were confused, uncertain of what to do next.

He knew that he had to make a connection with them—with each of them. But surely, if anyone could do that, *he* could.

After all, he had served with them already, in the not-so-distant future. He had come to know what motivated them, what made them defy the odds in situation after situation.

With that in mind, he now asked himself what sort of words were most likely to assuage their uncertainty. And, even more quickly than he might have hoped, the answer came to him.

He wouldn't try to win them over with abstract concepts of duty and survival. He would appeal to their pride in their abilities, to their sense of loyalty, to their hearts—and then he would hope for the best.

"You all have doubts about me," he acknowledged in stentorian tones. "About one another . . . about this ship. Unfortunately, I do not have the time to dispel them. All I can say is that, even though we've only been together for a short time, I know that you are the finest crew in the fleet."

At any rate, he had their attention. Each bridge officer was gazing at him intently now, weighing his or her assessment of him against the incredible and daring nature of his request.

"I would gladly trust any one of you with my life," the captain told them. "I would do so in any circumstance, at any place and time, without reservation." He looked into their eyes, hoping he'd accomplished what he needed to—but he couldn't be sure. "I can only hope," he entreated, "that you have that same trust in me . . . that you are able to make the leap of faith I am asking of you, regardless of the consequences."

For a time, there was silence on the bridge. Glances were exchanged, consensuses reached. Then, almost as one, the entire bridge contingent started working at their various tasks.

That was their answer. Not a cheer of approval, not a

roaring vote of confidence, but a simple demonstration of professionalism that spoke more loudly than voices ever could.

Picard was touched. He smiled with satisfaction. The team had come together at last, hadn't it? And not a moment too soon.

CHAPTER 24

Picard watched his bridge officers go into action like a well-oiled machine.

"Shields up," Tasha told him. "Maximum strength."

"Boosting field integrity on the warp nacelles," advised Worf. "We may encounter unexpected stress once we enter the anomaly."

"I am preparing to initiate a static warp shell," said Data.

"Course laid in, sir," called O'Brien.

Troi glanced at the monitor built into her armrest. "All decks report ready, Captain."

Picard surveyed his crew. He was proud of them. Damned proud.

"All right, Chief O'Brien." He sat down in his seat and leaned back. "Take us into . . ."

* * *

222

". . . the anomaly."

"Captain," said Data, swiveling in his seat. "I have an idea."

Picard wondered at the android's timing—until he realized that he was in the present again. "Yes, Mr. Data. What is it?"

"Sir, if we take the ship to the center of the anomaly and create a static warp shell . . ."

The captain saw where he was headed. "It could repair the barrier and collapse the anomaly."

The android seemed surprised. "Yes, sir."

Picard nodded. "I must tell you, Mr. Data—you're a clever man in any time period."

Data tilted his head slightly. "Thank you, sir. It is kind of you to say so."

Returning his attention to the viewscreen, the captain said, "Lay in a course to the center of the anomaly. Prepare to initiate a static warp shell."

The temporal shifts were coming so fast and furious now, he knew it would only be a matter of time before he . . .

. . . shifted into one of the other time periods.

Sure enough, in the blink of an eye, the image on the viewscreen had changed. The anomaly had diminished to almost nothing—alerting Picard to the fact that he was now in the future.

"The other two *Enterprise*s," he announced to all and sundry. "They're on their way."

Riker nodded. "Very well." Turning to the officer at conn, he said, "Ensign Genovese . . . take us in."

The *Enterprise* began moving toward the anomaly. Closer . . . and closer still . . . until the light dampers in the viewscreen could barely handle the level of illumination.

Picard swallowed. After all this, he hoped that he hadn't miscalculated somehow. The Irumodic syndrome wouldn't let him live all that much longer, but all those around him had plenty of time left.

La Forge had a family. Data had his students. Riker was a key man in the Starfleet hierarchy.

He didn't want to be the death of them—especially if it was all for . . .

. . . nothing.

Without warning, he found himself back in the past. This *Enterprise,* too, was headed into the anomaly.

His bridge officers were tense, even afraid, as they approached the unknown. But that didn't stop them from following his orders.

Closer . . . closer . . . into the Valley of Death? Or Salvation? They would find out soon enough.

O'Brien shifted in his chair. "We're entering the leading edge of the anomaly, sir."

"All hands brace for impact!" called the captain.

The ship rocked violently. All around the bridge, lights flickered. Deck plates shrieked with the strain.

"The temporal energy's interfering with main power," reported Tasha. "Switching to auxiliary . . ."

Another jolt, worse than the first . . .

* * *

. . . and before Picard could recover, he was in the present again. In this time period, the anomaly had already filled the viewscreen.

"Report!" roared Riker.

The ship was shuddering, a hint that the forces it strove against might simply be too powerful for it. Lights died and came alive again all over the bridge. They were pushing the *Enterprise* to her limits.

"I'm having trouble keeping the impulse engines on-line!" yelled Geordi. "We've got power fluctuations all across the board!"

"Maintain course and speed!" shouted the captain. He turned to his second officer. "Mr. Data, how long until we reach the center?"

The android hung on as the ship lurched again beneath them. "Another thirty seconds at least, sir."

Picard turned back to the viewscreen . . .

. . . where the anomaly didn't quite fill the screen. But then, why should it? In this future era, it was smaller, and they hadn't quite entered it yet.

As they got closer, Picard felt the deck tremble and hugged one of his armrests. His foresight was rewarded as the *Enterprise* bucked and heaved, throwing several crewmen to the deck.

This wasn't the place for an old man, he acknowledged ruefully. This wasn't the place for *anyone*. And yet, what choice did they have?

"We've entered the anomaly," called Gaines.

* * *

As if to underline the statement, Data looked over his shoulder and said, "We are approaching the focal point, sir."

Of course, this wasn't the Data of the future. It was the Data of the past, doggedly manning his ops station as they fought their way to the heart of the sprawling, seething anomaly.

"Ten seconds," the android announced. "Nine. Eight . . ."

Gritting his teeth, the captain watched his officers make adjustment after adjustment, utilizing every strategy they knew to keep the *Enterprise* on course and her engines on-line.

"Seven. Six. Five . . ." continued Data.

A little longer now. That was all he asked. A few more seconds and they would at least have a fighting chance.

The android went on with his countdown. "Four. Three. Two . . ."

And then they'd *done* it. They'd reached the center of the anomaly.

"One," called Data.

The onslaught of temporal energies was even fiercer here; they could barely keep their feet, much less concentrate on their controls. Up on the viewscreen, there was a pure, white light, as intense as the dawn of creation and unblemished by the merest hint of color.

Picard cried out, "Initiate warp shell!"

An island of calm in a sea of confusion, the android labored to comply with the captain's order . . .

* * *

. . . and called back, "Initiating static warp shell—
now."

Suddenly, things had changed. Picard was back in the
present, where a tiny bead of perspiration was making its
way down Will Riker's face, and where Ensign Calan's
shoulders were bunched together so tightly it hurt just to
look at her.

The present . . . where Data was single-mindedly applying himself to his lonely task, and where the captain
himself wished desperately to remain for a little while.

Then again, he thought, for that very reason it
probably . . .

. . . wouldn't last.

He looked around, aware that he'd shifted again. But
where this time? Or rather, *when?*

The blinding brilliance put out by the viewscreen
didn't allow him to see much. But judging by the
cloudiness of his mind, it was the future.

Another jolt, and Picard was half-torn out of his seat.
As he dragged himself back in, he heard Riker's voice. It
cut through the clamor like a klaxon.

"Is it having any effect?" he asked.

Another switch—this time, to the past. The captain
could tell by his uniform, even if he couldn't see much
else.

As in the other two time frames, the ship was tossing
like a leaf in a hurricane. Beside him, Troi's eyes were
wide with barely contained fear.

"Something is happening within the anomaly," Data declared from his post at ops. "A new subspace barrier appears to be forming. . . ."

Tasha cried out, "Captain! Sensors are picking up two other *ships . . . !*"

Everyone's eyes were drawn to the viewscreen, where they saw a spectacle that seemed to defy reality. In the midst of the roiling display of temporal energies, Picard could see the ghostly images of two other *Enterprise*s.

The ships were drifting in the anomaly, remarkably close to each other. In fact, as the captain peered at them from the command center, they actually appeared to be moving *through* each other.

His mouth went dry as he . . .

. . . joined the bridge contingent in the present.

Like everyone else, he was peering at the viewscreen —where two other *Enterprise*s were being tossed about in the anomaly's temporal maelstrom.

As his mind reeled from the acceleration of his time-shifting, Picard could scarcely . . .

. . . remember where he was—until he turned and saw the gray-bearded Admiral Riker sitting next to him. Like everyone else, he was fascinated by the sight of two other *Enterprise*s on the viewscreen.

The past and the present had finally caught up with them, at least here in the confines of the anomaly . . .

* * *

. . . where the present and the future seemed to have met them head-on.

"It appears to be working," shouted Tasha, intent on her tactical monitors. "The anomaly is beginning to collapse. I think that . . ."

She hesitated, and he turned. For a moment, their eyes met, and he knew that the news wouldn't be good.

"Sir," she cried, her brow creased with concern, "the temporal energy is disrupting our warp containment system!"

Picard swore. That was the only problem they couldn't take in stride, the only puzzle they couldn't find a solution for.

"We must eject the core!" thundered Worf.

"No!" bellowed the captain. "We have to maintain the static warp shell for as long as possible!"

The ship staggered and quaked under the temporal onslaught. Picard couldn't look directly at the viewscreen, lest it blind him.

"I'm losing containment!" barked Tasha, her eyes wide with expectation. "I can't stop it. It's going to—"

Back in the present, Picard's eyes were fixed on the viewscreen. Through the chaos of the anomaly, he saw one of the two other *Enterprise*s engulfed in a conflagration of flames and debris. And having just been on board the doomed vessel, he knew which one it was.

Filled with a sense of immeasurable loss, he wished he had time to mourn staunch, loyal Tasha and the young, headstrong Worf . . . or Troi of that time frame, or

O'Brien. As it was, he could only do his best to make sure they hadn't died for nothing.

Quickly, he turned to Geordi, reluctant to make the same mistake twice. "Transfer emergency power to the antimatter containment system!"

The chief engineer worked frantically at his console. "I'm trying, sir . . . but there's a lot of interference. . . ."

The ship lurched and swung, jerking them out of their seats. As the captain got to his feet, he heard Data say, "The warp shells are definitely having an effect, sir. The anomaly is beginning to collapse."

"Maintain position!" Picard bellowed. "At all costs, maintain position! Mr. La Forge—"

As he clung to his armrests with aged, blue-veined hands, Picard could see the *Enterprise* of the present go up in a ball of fiery energies. The significance of it hit him square in the chest, with the impact of a phaser beam set to stun.

Will and Deanna, cut down in their prime. The same with Worf and Data and Geordi, never to know what life might have had in store for them. And Beverly . . . who would never have to put up with a husband named Picard.

"Damn," he muttered, reeling at the thought of it. Then, driven by curiosity and dread, he turned . . .

And saw them all around him. All of them except Deanna, of course. Beverly and Riker and Worf, La Forge and Data . . . they were all very much alive, here in the future.

But how could that be? How could they still exist when they had watched their younger selves perish? Their continued presence here defied the laws of time and space.

Then he remembered something that someone had said . . . in the observation lounge, perhaps. In the present . . . or was it the past? Something about a lack of causality among the three timelines.

In other words, each *Enterprise could* have existed independently of the others, unrelated by conditions and events. And judging by the way things had turned out, that was exactly the way it had been.

Abruptly, Picard caught sight of something in the corner of his eye. Glancing to one side of the command center, he felt himself blanch.

There was a tall figure standing there in black robes, with a scythe resting on his shoulder and an hourglass in his hand. At first glance, he thought it was truly the Grim Reaper.

Then, as the foreboding figure turned to look at him, he saw a familiar face in the depths of its cowl—and realized that it was Q. Apparently, the entity had come to torment them in their darkest hour.

As Q smiled, Picard glared at him with overpowering hatred. How could anyone derive so much pleasure from a lesser being's misery? How could he be so callous, so cruel?

"Two down, Jean-Luc," remarked Q. "And one to go . . ."

Picard swallowed his anger. He couldn't afford the distraction. "Not now, Q!"

He turned to Data, who was still at his station. Gathering his strength, he yelled over the rising din, "Report!"

"The anomaly is nearly collapsed . . ." said the android, the calmness of his voice belying the urgency of his statement.

"We're losing containment . . ." warned Geordi.

"We have to hang on!" cried Picard, his voice cracking. "We have to hang on as long as we can!"

Q leaned closer to the captain. Apparently, no one else on the bridge could see or hear him.

"Good-bye, Jean-Luc," he said in earnest tones. "I'll miss you, you know. You did have a great deal of potential . . . of entertainment value. But as you can see, *all good things* must come to an end."

Geordi shook his head, not liking what he saw on his monitor. "Containment field at critical! Captain, I'm losing it—"

Picard had heard those words before. As he braced himself for the ensuing explosion . . . for failure on a cosmic scale, for the end of things, for the cloying embrace of chaos . . . something different happened.

The *Enterprise* didn't explode at all. It hung there, frozen in a moment of time, with the bridge crew and his comrades exchanging final glances. And as that moment stretched out as no moment had a right to, the anomaly collapsed inward on itself.

The captain saw it on the viewscreen—or rather, an aspect of it, because they were too close to get any real perspective on the spectacle. It was as if the physical representations of temporal disorder were folding in on themselves like an accordion . . . completely and infinitely, finally and irrevocably.

Of course, for Picard and the others, the outcome was the same: death . . . destruction . . . annihilation. But maybe, just maybe, they had saved the race of humanoids who had given birth to them . . . the hopeful, hopeless beings who had climbed from their murky pools one day in order to get a glimpse of the stars.

In the end, all was white. And silent. And strangely, wonderfully, hideously at rest.

CHAPTER 25

"**J**ean-Luc?"

Picard looked up and found himself standing alone in a courtroom. And not just *any* courtroom, but the twenty-first-century chamber in which Q had tried him seven years ago.

Of course, some things had changed. He was dressed in his "present-day" uniform. The gallery of leering, hungry-eyed gawkers was gone. . . .

And though the captain had distinctly heard Q's voice, Q himself was nowhere to be seen.

"Up here," said the voice. This time, it sounded more than a little exasperated.

He looked up—and saw Q descending, as if from the ether, on his floating cushion. He was dressed in his flowing judge's robes again.

Q studied him. "The Continuum didn't think you had it in you, Jean-Luc. But I knew you could."

Picard felt his heart leap. "Are you saying it worked? Did we shut down the anomaly?"

Judge Q shook his head. "Is that all this meant to you? Just another spatial anomaly . . . just another day at the office?"

The captain took an angry step toward his nemesis. "Q," he rumbled, "did it *work* or didn't it?"

Q held his hands out, as if the answer had been in front of him all along. "You're here, aren't you? You're talking to me, aren't you? Albeit, I'll admit, without making much sense."

Picard considered the essence of the remark. He *was* here. He *was* talking. Then . . . could it be they had won? But . . .

"What about my crew?" he asked. "In fact, what about all three of my crews?"

Again, Q took on that expression of derision. "Is that all you can think about?" He spoke mockingly, imitating the captain's questions. " 'The anomaly . . . my crew . . . my ship.' I suppose you're worried about your damned fish, too."

The entity snorted. "Well, if it puts your mind at ease, you've saved humanity once again. Congratulations are in order. Hip, hip, hooray." Slowly, scornfully, Q clapped his hands in feigned celebration. "But I must say," he continued, "I'm a little disappointed in you."

Picard chuckled dryly. "Oh, no . . . not that. Heaven forfend."

Q's expression hardened. "You really don't know what just happened, do you?" he asked, his voice taking on a dangerous edge. "You're still the same primitive little man I met seven years ago. Same limited vision, same inflexible perceptions of the universe." He harrumphed. "I never should have been so generous."

"Generous?" echoed the captain, tilting his head to show his skepticism. "In what way?"

Q was clearly angry now. "That's right, Picard. *Generous*. It was my generosity that enabled you to travel through time. If I hadn't stepped in and given you that chance—the opportunity to see what should have been obvious to you all along—you and your pitiful race would be deceased. Extinct. Kaput. Finito. Just another dead end along the evolutionary-chain highway."

The captain had no reason to disbelieve him. Though Q often dealt in half-truths and exaggerations, bald-faced lies just weren't his style.

And if he *had* endowed Picard with the ability to time-skip . . . if it was his intervention that had given mankind a shot at survival . . . then the captain's duty was clear.

Putting his animosity aside, he smiled . . . looked Q in his baleful eyes . . . and said, "Thank you."

The Q entity looked back at him, uncharacteristically off-balance. "What . . . did you say?" he stammered.

"I won't tell you again," Picard replied. "But you're right—you did give me a chance. And I do appreciate it."

Q smiled back. "I will say this for you, Jean-Luc . . . you always have been full of surprises." He leaned forward on his floating cushion. "So surprise me again. Tell me you've taken something more away from this experience. Say you've expanded your horizons *just the tiniest, little bit.*"

The captain looked at the entity askance. What knowledge had he taken away from this? And why was it so important to Q that he'd learned something?

After all, he had accomplished what he'd needed to accomplish. He had done what was necessary to preserve his own kind.

Unless . . .

Suddenly, Picard saw what it had all been about. And he wasn't happy—not in the least. In fact, he felt more humiliated than ever.

"I saw my way out of a paradox," the captain responded. "And in the process, I broke free of my preconceptions of time and space. That's what this was all about, wasn't it?" He grunted, amazed at the Continuum's audacity.

Q's eyes narrowed. "Now you're catching on, *mon capitaine.* For one split second, your mind was open to possibilities and ideas you'd never dreamt of. But it was only the beginning."

Picard wanted to be angry—but somehow, he couldn't be. As twisted as Q's methods were, his motives seemed almost . . . altruistic.

"You think of yourself as an explorer," Q expanded, warming to his subject. "And yet, how little you understand the universe you live in."

He gestured ever so slightly, and the captain's head was suddenly full of images and concepts he couldn't begin to comprehend. It was staggering . . . overwhelming.

Q went on, his voice a distant drone. "The real voyage of exploration has yet to begin, Jean-Luc . . . a voyage vastly unlike any other in your experience. And it has nothing to do with mapping star systems and charting nebulae. It's a voyage of perceptions . . . of thoughts . . . of moments and possibilities . . ."

Just as Picard thought he was beginning to see, the images vanished. It left him feeling empty . . . and terribly alone, like someone who has been cut off from the very thing that defined him.

"Well," Q told him, "maybe you're not quite ready yet. But you seem to have demonstrated a certain aptitude for higher learning. Perhaps someday, you'll get the picture." He dusted off his judge's robes. "In any case, I'll be here watching . . . and waiting. And if you're very, very lucky, I'll drop by to say hello from time to time."

Q was becoming translucent, immaterial. Already, the details of the courtroom were visible through him.

"Until we meet again, *mon capitaine*. In the meantime, you really should get some clothes on. You'll catch your death of cold."

As the last of his adversary faded away, Picard reached out . . .

. . . and found himself stepping out of a turbolift, dressed in nothing but his bathrobe.

Worf and Deanna were standing there in the corridor, looking at him in surprise. It took the captain a moment to realize what had happened.

Q had deposited him back at the beginning of his adventure . . . if one could call it that. This was the point at which he had pleaded with the counselor for help, and then—

Yes. And *then*.

This time, however, it would be different. After all, he wasn't staggering around, claiming vague recollections of his initial experiences in the past and the future.

This time, his memories were clear and complete. He remembered all that had happened, from his meeting with Geordi in the vineyard at Labarre to his final assault on the anomaly in all three time periods. And Q himself had told him that his gambit had ultimately succeeded.

Because of that, events could not help but pursue a different course. Or could they?

A specter of doubt raised its head. What if Q had plunked him down at some other point in time . . . a point that only superficially resembled the beginning of his time trek?

What if there was something about his test that was still incomplete? What if, through some cruel turn of events, there was still some aspect of the puzzle left to be solved?

Deanna stared at him with concern in her lovely dark eyes. "Captain, are you all right?"

His heart banging against his ribs, Picard turned to the Klingon. "Lieutenant . . . what's the date?"

Worf wasn't sure what was going on—but he answered anyway. "Stardate four-seven-nine-eight-eight."

Stardate *four-seven-nine-eight-eight*. The exact same day and time on which his time-shifting escapade had begun.

The captain was overwhelmed with relief. He laughed out loud, not caring about the wary look that went back and forth between Deanna and Worf. For the moment, not caring about anything . . . except the fact that he was back where he belonged.

"Is something wrong, sir?" asked the counselor.

Picard shook his head. "Not at all. In fact, I think I'll go back to bed. I could really do with some sleep."

And with that, he stepped back inside the turbolift compartment. As the doors closed, the last thing he saw was the querulous expressions on the faces of his officers.

CHAPTER 26

Captain's Log, Supplemental. All is once again right with the galaxy. Starfleet Command reports no unusual activity along the Neutral Zone, nor is there any sign of the temporal anomaly. What's more, it would appear I am the only member of the crew to retain any knowledge of the events I experienced—though I've seen fit to brief my senior staff on them.

Crusher looked at Riker. As always, his expression was unreadable. He had the best poker face she'd ever seen.

"Well?" he asked.

There was a note of confidence in his voice. Was it a bluff, intended to scare her off? Or was he trying to make it seem like a bluff, so as to draw her in even further?

The doctor took another look at her hand. She had a straight to the ten. A damned good hand, by any account. But she'd lost with better. And usually, it had been to Riker.

Still, she'd come this far. A high percentage of the plastic chips in the center of the table were hers. And if she didn't go in, the first officer would win without showing what he held.

Crusher couldn't let him do that. Win or lose, she had to see what was in the cards.

"All right," the doctor said finally. "I'll see you."

She had only ten chips left, but she pushed them all into the existing pot. Then she eyed the bearded man and revealed her hand.

"Can you beat a straight?"

Still, Riker gave no indication of whether he'd won or lost. One by one, he placed his cards down on the table. A four. Another four. A deuce. A second deuce. And finally . . . a third deuce.

"Full boat," he announced, unable to keep from cracking a smile. "My apologies, Doctor."

"No need," Crusher advised him. "As usual, I've got only myself to blame." Pushing her chair back, she got up from the poker table.

"That's it?" asked Worf.

"For me it is," she confirmed.

Geordi regarded her sympathetically. "There's always next time," he suggested.

The doctor scowled. "I suppose. It's a good thing I've got my medical career to fall back on, because I certainly couldn't make it as an interplanetary cardsharp."

Riker grinned as he organized his chips, which easily constituted the largest collection on the table. He was obviously quite pleased with himself, and he wasn't bothering to conceal it.

Geordi turned to Worf. "That's four hands in a row," he observed. "How does he do it?"

The Klingon swore under his breath. "I would like to know myself, Commander."

The first officer chuckled to himself. "Simple," he said. "I cheat."

Data had begun to collect the cards. Abruptly, his head snapped up. There was a shocked expression on his face.

"I'm kidding," the exec assured him. "Really."

As if he'd never heard the remark, the android went back to shuffling the deck again.

Crusher moved to an empty chair off to the side and sank into it. It was just as comfortable as it looked.

"You know," she said after a while, "I've been thinking . . ."

Geordi cast a glance at her. "About what?"

She smiled to herself. "About all the things the captain told us about the future. The things he said about us . . . about our relationships . . . the way we changed and drifted apart." She paused. "Why would he tell us what's going to happen?"

The engineer shrugged. "It *does* go against everything we've heard about not polluting the timeline. . . ."

They pondered the question for a moment. As was often the case, Data was the first to come to a conclusion.

"I believe," he said, "that this situation is unique."

"How so?" asked Riker.

The android turned to him. "Since the temporal anomaly did not occur," he reasoned, "and *will* not occur, there have already been changes in the way this timeline is unfolding. The future we experience will undoubtedly be different from the one the captain encountered."

The first officer nodded. "Maybe that's why he told us. Knowing what that future could bring . . . gives us a chance to change things *now.*"

"So those events don't have a chance to take place," Geordi elaborated.

"Right," confirmed Riker. He gave Worf a meaningful look. "And in the case of *some* of those events, we should take *extra* care to see that they don't happen."

The Klingon nodded in appreciation. "Agreed," he said.

They heard the sound of chimes, announcing the presence of someone at the door.

"Come on in," replied the first officer.

As the doors parted, Troi was revealed. She looked around the table.

"Am I too late?" she asked.

"No," said Riker. "Not at all, Deanna. In fact, I was just getting up. Take my seat."

With that, he got up and offered her his chair—which happened to be next to Worf's. Fully cognizant of the significance of the gesture, the Betazoid sat down.

"Thanks," she told the first officer.

Riker smiled at her. "My pleasure."

Crusher saw Worf glance at the counselor, then at the first officer. There was no need to speak the words that went with his sentiments. At least, not right now.

"Four-handed poker?" asked Troi, breaking the silence. She looked up again at Riker. "Can I convince you to sit down again?"

The first officer shook his head. "I think I've worn out my welcome. Deal me out for a couple of hands and I might reconsider."

She turned to Crusher. "Bev?"

The doctor held up a hand. "Not me," she declined. "I took enough of a beating before you got here."

The chimes sounded again. "Come," said Riker.

Crusher couldn't guess who else might want to join the game. All the regulars were already here.

As a result, she was quite surprised when she saw the captain standing there in the corridor. Everyone sat up at attention as he entered.

The first officer looked concerned. "Sir—is there a problem?"

Picard shook his head. "No, no problem at all. I just thought I might . . . join you this evening. That is, if there's room . . ."

Glances were exchanged. And smiles.

"There's *plenty* of room," said Riker, speaking for all of them. "In fact, it looks to me like there's a seat next to Data . . . the one Dr. Crusher just abandoned."

The captain looked at his chief medical officer. "A run of bad luck?" he asked politely.

She shrugged. "Maybe it'll change," she hoped out loud.

As Picard sat down, the android gave him the deck of cards. "Would you care to deal, sir?"

The captain seemed pleased. "Oh . . . thank you." He started to shuffle the cards. "You know, I should have done this a long time ago. I was quite a cardplayer in my youth, you know."

Troi leaned forward slightly. "You were always welcome here, sir."

He nodded. "Yes," he said. "I know."

Crusher could see that his experience had left him

MICHAEL JAN FRIEDMAN

with a new appreciation for life . . . and for people. Especially *these* people, who were more like a family to him than a collection of colleagues.

"Sometimes," Picard went on, "you lose sight of the things that are truly important. I hope I won't make that mistake again."

As he glanced at each of them in turn, the doctor could see the brightness in his eyes that betrayed his feelings for them. And also, perhaps, for a certain blond security officer who was no longer with them. Then, a little embarrassed, he began dealing the cards.

"So," he said, regaining command of himself. "Five-card stud, nothing wild. The sky's the limit."

Crusher looked at him . . . and still couldn't help but wonder. Would she and the captain marry one day? And if they did, would it end in divorce, as in the timeline he had experienced?

Would Picard fall victim to Irumodic syndrome—or escape it? Would he remain in Starfleet, or go back to Earth to become a vintner?

Would Troi and Worf fall in love, as it appeared they would? And if they did, what would come of it?

Would the Romulan Empire fall? Would a rift form between the Federation and the Klingons? What role would the manipulative Cardassians play? The Tholians? The Ferengi?

And so on. There were any number of questions, none of which could accurately be answered without a crystal ball. And it was just as well, wasn't it?

Because none of them really wanted to know the future. Each one of them wanted the chance to mold it, for better or worse, in his or her own two hands.

That was the way it had always been, since the birth of

man. And though she couldn't deny her curiosity, she was glad that was the way it would continue to be . . .

At least, for a *while*.

Q had never been a one-eyed jack before. As it happened, he rather liked it, particularly because it gave him a jack's-eye view of his favorite human sparring partner.

Picard was frowning at him—and not because he knew that Q was posing as a card in his hand. The problem was, the other four cards were all clubs, and Q was the jack of hearts.

No doubt the captain would be discarding him at his earliest opportunity. Casting him off like a used dishrag. Tossing him in the huge, echoing wastebasket of life.

But that was all right. Q could always turn up elsewhere. And unless the Continuum decided to curb him again in some way, he most certainly would.

After all, no one entertained him quite as much as Picard did. No one did so much with so little. And no one was so good at reminding the entity of what it was like to be a human being.

He was tempted to turn around and stick his tongue out at the captain, but—for once—he held himself in check. After all, he didn't want Picard to take him for granted. Having said good-bye to the man, it was much too early to say hello again.

Glancing over Picard's shoulder at the ever-annoying Dr. Crusher, he could feel his stomach churning as he considered her questions about the future—and that was no easy feat for mere pasteboard. Marriage. Love. Divorce. It was all so incredibly *mundane*.

Or was that just because he knew how it was all going to turn out? Might it not be a little more interesting if one was limited to knowing the past and the present, and restricted from peeking into the future?

He tried to imagine what that would be like—and found he couldn't. After all, his consciousness spanned time and space—and then some. It would be like asking a human not to think.

And what was all this rubbish about molding one's own future? Free will was an amusing notion, but to actually believe in it . . . was there no end to the gullibility of these creatures?

Uh-oh. The captain was reaching for him. Plucking him out from the company of the other cards. Tossing him facedown on the table.

Too bad, thought Q, with a sadness that he felt as deeply as he was capable of feeling anything. He'd rather enjoyed being part of the game.